Thornes Classic Short Stories

D1807783

SHORT STORIES

by

EDGAR ALLAN POE

EDITED BY MIKE ROYSTON

SERIES EDITOR: MIKE ROYSTON

Stanley Thornes (Publishers) Ltd

Hop-Frog first published 1849
The Tell-Tale Heart first published 1843
The Masque of the Red Death first published 1842
The Cask of Amontillado first published 1846
'Thou Art the Man' first published 1844

This edition first published in 1997 by:
Stanley Thornes (Publishers) Ltd
Ellenborough House
Wellington Street
CHELTENHAM GL50 1YW
England

97 98 99 00 01 / 10 9 8 7 6 5 4 3 2 1

A catalogue record for this book is available from the British Library.

ISBN 0–7487–3096–6

Acknowledgements

The author and publishers are grateful to the following for permission to reproduce illustrations and photographs:
Hulton Getty Picture Collection pp. 4, 5 (bottom) ● Mary Evans Picture Library pp. 2, 3 (both), 5 (top), 6.

Typeset by Tech-Set, Gateshead
Illustrated by Susan Hutchison
With thanks to Sue Whimster for her editorial work on this book.
Printed and bound in Great Britain at T J Press (Padstow) Ltd, Cornwall

Contents

How to use this book

This book contains five short stories by Edgar Allan Poe. It is designed so that you can read the stories on your own, or share your reading with others. Whichever way you read, the stories have been chosen above all to be *enjoyed*.

The Introduction contains:

- a brief account of the writer's life. This gives you an impression of the kind of person he was and outlines the most important things that happened to him during his lifetime.

- a background to the stories, in words and pictures. This tells you about the kind of stories they are and helps you to approach your reading of them in an informed way.

To help you get the most from them, the stories have been presented in a particular way. They contain the following features:

- boxes at the beginning of each story, and at other key points, which suggest what you should look out for as you read.

- a glossary at the foot of every page giving the meanings of words you may find unfamiliar.

- a commentary summarising what is happening on each page of the story, to help you follow it as you read.

During each story, you will now and again come across a 'Pause for playback' section. This contains brief questions to highlight important points in the part of the story you have just read. You can make up your own mind about the 'answers'. They do not have to be written down.

After each story, there is a Study guide. This contains activities designed to help you form an understanding of the story as a whole. Some activities are for small groups, some are for pairs, and some for doing by yourself.

At the end of the book, you will find an Overview section. This asks you to think further about how the stories are written and to make some comparisons between them.

Enjoy your reading!

Introduction

Edgar Allan Poe's brief life was filled with misfortune. Born in 1809 in Boston, Massachusetts, he was an orphan before the age of 3. Both his parents were travelling actors, a hard and unrewarding life. Soon after Poe's birth his father disappeared without trace, and in 1811 his mother died in Richmond, Virginia.

Poe was fostered – but never legally adopted – by a Richmond merchant, John Allan: hence his middle name. Relations between them were always strained. Poe was highly strung and rebellious; his foster-father was stern. He took the boy on a five-year trip to England, during which Poe went to school in Stoke Newington on the outskirts of London. On their return to Virginia, Poe started university.

His career there did not last long. In his first year, Poe's gambling debts had grown so large that, after a violent quarrel, John Allan disowned him. With no one else to pay his fees, Poe was forced to leave university. At the age of 19 he joined the Army, finally becoming a cadet at the US Military Academy at West Point, New York. Here again he ran into trouble. He was court-martialled for refusing to obey orders and had to leave in disgrace.

Poe (right) with friends at the University of Virginia in the 1830s

By now Poe, aged 22, had decided to become a writer. He tried journalism, working on newspapers in Richmond and Philadelphia, and succeeded in having several 'sensational' stories published in magazines. But Poe was more interested in becoming a poet. He had also become a serious drinker, which left him quarrelsome, violent and often penniless.

In 1836, Poe married his cousin, Virginia. He was 27; she was 13. They were desperately poor and had to live with Virginia's mother in a small house in Baltimore. Poe's stories continued to appear in magazines throughout the Southern States, but he made very little money from them. Only in 1846, when *The Raven and Other Poems* was published, did he gain any real recognition as a writer.

Virginia Poe

An engraving of Edgar Allan Poe

Shortly after, Virginia died of tuberculosis, aged 24. Poe was not only broken-hearted; his young wife's death also unhinged his mind. He began to suffer frequent bouts of insanity. Some of his 'darkest' stories of horror and madness belong to this period of his life. It was not to last much longer, however. After a drinking session extending over several weeks, Poe died in October, 1849. He was just 40 years old.

BACKGROUND TO THE STORIES

Publication: difficulties and debts

For more than a century, Poe's stories have been among the most popular in the world. In his own lifetime, though, the hard-working editor of *The Southern Literary Messenger* – annual salary, $600 – found American publishers reluctant to publish them at all. All five stories in this book first appeared in different periodicals. None of them was printed by the journal which employed him.

In 1840, the near-penniless author finally saw his stories collected in *Tales of the Grotesque and the Arabesque*. His 'fee' was ten free copies. He got no money at all. Poe wrote a six-line letter of complaint to the publishers. More free copies came, but still no money. Ironically, a century after his death, Poe's letter of complaint was sold at auction for $3,000.

His debts can hardly have been eased by the fee he earned for one of his most famous stories, *The Fall of the House of Usher* (1839). It fetched him the princely sum of $10.

An illustration drawn in about 1845 for The Fall of the House of Usher

Poe's influence

All this is more remarkable in view of the indebtedness to Edgar Allan Poe of later writers. Poe did not 'invent' the horror story. He did, however, establish his own *form* of it so strongly that modern writers such as Mervyn Peake (in his *Gormenghast* books) and Stephen King freely admit Poe's influence. It is scarcely imaginable that Robert Louis Stevenson could have produced *The Strange Case of Dr Jekyll and Mr Hyde* without such stories about 'split personality' as Poe's *William Wilson* (1839) behind him.

A twentieth-century illustration for The Purloined Letter

Poe has a strong claim to have originated the detective thriller. His master-detective, C. Auguste Dupin, in stories like *The Murders in the Rue Morgue* (1841) and *The Purloined Letter* (1844), solves crimes with precisely the same suave logic as Arthur Conan Doyle's Sherlock Holmes. Less well known is the fact that Poe was the first writer of what might be called the 'science-fiction' short story: see, for example, *A Descent Into the Maelstrom* or *Some Words With a Mummy*. Jules Verne, author of *Journey to the Centre of the Earth* (1864) and *20,000 Leagues Under the Sea* (1869), acknowledged Poe as an inspiration and a model.

Gothic terror

'Gothic', as applied to literature, is a slippery word that has nothing to do with the Goths. Think of a typical Hammer House of Horror film. As often as not, it will take place in the vaguely distant past and be set in a ruined castle. Here a brutal villain (probably deformed) pursues his evil ends. He will have a strong taste for violence and torture. Many of the rest of the cast are – or become – ghosts and phantoms.

Had you lived between 1760 and 1820, you could have read book after book with exactly these Gothic ingredients in them. You would have had your hair raised by Horace Walpole's *The Castle of Otranto* (1764), your blood curdled by Mrs Ann Radcliffe's *The Mysteries of Udolpho* (1794), your pulse quickened by Matthew Lewis's *The Monk* (1796), and your spine chilled by Mary Shelley's *Frankenstein* (1818).

An illustration from The Raven, *written in 1845*

All of these English novels were known to an American adolescent named E. A. Poe. Just as influential on him were the 'terror stories' published in *Blackwood's Magazine* between 1821 and 1827. Their titles read like a catalogue of Hammer films – 'The Murderer's Last Night', 'The Iron Shroud', 'The Suicide' and 'The Buried Alive'. As you read Poe's stories in this volume, see how many of the titles just listed could act as sub-titles for *his*.

The uniqueness of Poe

Why are Poe's stories worth reading today when the *Blackwood's* ones have been long forgotten? Perhaps because, as a master of atmosphere, he could create 'terror' that does not seem too far-fetched but real and familiar to us. Poe was a tormented man. Many readers think that he has the power to torment their own imaginations with what he himself called 'the terror of the soul'. See if you agree with them.

A Victorian engraving of the unnerving effects of reading Gothic novels late at night

OTHER RECOMMENDED STORIES BY EDGAR ALLAN POE

The Fall of the House of Usher

The Pit and the Pendulum

Manuscript Found in a Bottle

The Gold-Bug

The Murders in the Rue Morgue

The Mystery of Marie Roget

The Purloined Letter

Some Words with a Mummy

A Descent Into the Maelstrom

King Pest

The Man that was Used Up

William Wilson

The Facts in the Case of M. Valdemar

You can find these stories in *Tales of Mystery and Imagination* (Longman, 1993) and *The Complete Tales and Poems of Edgar Allan Poe* (Penguin, 1982).

HOP-FROG

Look out for...
- **what we discover about Hop-Frog and his background.**
- **the cruel way in which the king treats Hop-Frog and Trippetta.**
- **Hop-Frog's idea for providing the king with an entertainment.**

I never knew anyone so keenly alive to a joke as the king was. He seemed to live only for joking. To tell a good story of the joke kind, and to tell it well, was the surest road to his favour. Thus it happened that his seven ministers were all noted for their accomplishments as jokers. They all took after the king, too, in being large, corpulent, oily men, as well as inimitable jokers. Whether people grow fat by joking, or whether there is something in fat itself which predisposes to a joke, I have never been quite able to determine; but certain it is that a lean joker is a *rara avis in terris*.

About the refinements, or, as he called them, the 'ghosts' of wit, the king troubled himself very little. He had an especial admiration for *breadth* in a jest, and would often put up with *length*, for the sake of it. Over-niceties wearied him. He would have preferred Rabelais's 'Gargantua' to the 'Zadig' of Voltaire: and, upon the whole, practical jokes suited his taste far better than verbal ones.

At the date of my narrative, professing jesters had not altogether gone out of fashion at court. Several of the great continental 'powers' still retained their 'fools', who wore motley, with caps and bells, and who were expected to be

COMMENTARY

The story takes place in the past, at a time when kings employed jesters to keep them amused. The king in this story, along with his chief courtiers, likes nothing better than a good practical joke.

corpulent: very fat
inimitable: the best, most original
predisposes: leads a person towards
rara avis in terris: a rare bird on this earth
*Rabelais's 'Gargantua' to the 'Zadig' of
   Voltaire:* the first of these French
   authors wrote vulgar comedy; the
   second was more subtle
professing: professional
motley: a jester's costume

always ready with sharp witticisms, at a moment's notice, in consideration of the crumbs that fell from the royal table.

Our king, as a matter of course, retained his 'fool'. The fact is, he *required* something in the way of folly – if only to counterbalance the heavy wisdom of the seven wise men who were his ministers – not to mention himself.

His fool, or professional jester, was not *only* a fool, however. His value was trebled in the eyes of the king, by the fact of his being also a dwarf and a cripple. Dwarfs were as common at court, in those days, as fools; and many monarchs would have found it difficult to get through their days (days are rather longer at court than elsewhere) without both a jester to laugh *with*, and a dwarf to laugh *at*. But, as I have already observed, your jesters , in ninety-nine cases out of a hundred, are fat, round and unwieldy – so that it was no small source of self-gratulation with our king that, in Hop-Frog (this was the fool's name), he possessed a triplicate treasure in one person.

I believe the name 'Hop-Frog' was *not* that given to the dwarf by his sponsors at baptism, but it was conferred upon him, by general consent of the seven ministers, on account of his inability to walk as other men do. In fact, Hop-Frog could only get along by a sort of interjectional gait – something between a leap and a wriggle – a movement that afforded illimitable amusement, and of course consolation, to the king, for (notwithstanding the protuberance of his stomach and a constitutional swelling of the head) the king, by his whole court, was accounted a capital figure.

But although Hop-Frog, through the distortion of his legs, could move only with great pain and difficulty along a road or floor, the prodigious muscular power which nature seemed to have bestowed upon his arms, by way of compensation for deficiency in the lower limbs, enabled him to perform many feats of wonderful dexterity, where trees or ropes were in question, or anything else to climb. At such exercises he certainly much more resembled a squirrel, or a small monkey, than a frog.

I am not able to say, with precision, from what country Hop-Frog originally came. It was from some barbarous region, however, that no person had ever

counterbalance: provide relief from
unwieldy: clumsy
self-gratulation: self-congratulation
sponsors: godparents
interjectional gait: in a jerky way
illimitable: endless
protuberance: vast swelling
capital: splendid, excellent
prodigious: tremendous
dexterity: agility
barbarous: uncivilised

COMMENTARY
Hop-Frog is the king's jester. He is also a dwarf and a cripple, which is where his nickname comes from. Although his legs are almost useless to him, he possesses great strength in his arms and is an acrobatic climber.

heard of – a vast distance from the court of our king. Hop-Frog, and a young girl very little less dwarfish than himself (although of exquisite proportions, and a marvellous dancer), had been forcibly carried off from their respective homes in adjoining provinces, and sent as presents to the king, by one of his ever-victorious generals.

Under these circumstances, it is not to be wondered at that a close intimacy arose between the two little captives. Indeed, they soon became sworn friends. Hop-Frog, who, although he made a great deal of sport, was by no means popular, had it not in his power to render Trippetta many services; but *she*, on account of her grace and exquisite beauty (although a dwarf), was universally admired and petted: so she possessed much influence; and never failed to use it, whenever she could, for the benefit of Hop-Frog.

On some grand state occasion – I forget what – the king determined to have a masquerade; and whenever a masquerade, or anything of that kind, occurred at our court, then the talents of both Hop-Frog and Trippetta were sure to be called in play. Hop-Frog, in especial, was so inventive in the way of getting up pageants, suggesting novel characters, and arranging costumes for masked balls, that nothing could be done, it seems, without his assistance.

The night appointed for the *fête* had arrived. A gorgeous hall had been fitted up, under Trippetta's eye, with every kind of device which could possibly give *éclat* to a masquerade. The whole court was in a fever of expectation. As for costumes and characters, it might well be supposed that everybody had come to a decision on such points. Many had made up their minds (as to what *rôles* they should assume) a week, or even a month, in advance; and, in fact, there was not a particle of indecision anywhere – except in the case of the king and his seven ministers. Why *they* hesitated I never could tell, unless they did it by way of a joke. More probably, they found it difficult, on account of being so fat, to make up their minds. At all events, time flew; and, as a last resource, they sent for Trippetta and Hop-Frog.

When the two little friends obeyed the summons of the king, they found him sitting at his wine with the seven members of his cabinet council; but the

---

COMMENTARY

Hop-Frog and a female dwarf, Trippetta, were presents to the king from a far-away country. They have become the closest of friends. The king decides to hold a masked ball. Both Hop-Frog and Trippetta have an important part to play in helping to arrange it.

of exquisite proportions: physically graceful
intimacy: loving friendship
masquerade: a fancy dress ball, at which masks are worn
getting up pageants: devising plays and charades
eye: supervision
éclat: a showy splendour
a particle of indecision: the slightest doubt

monarch appeared to be in a very ill humour. He knew that Hop-Frog was not fond of wine; for it excited the poor cripple almost to madness; and madness is no comfortable feeling. But the king loved his practical jokes, and took pleasure in forcing Hop-Frog to drink and (as the king called it) 'to be merry'.

'Come here, Hop-Frog,' said he, as the jester and his friend entered the room: 'swallow this bumper to the health of your absent friends' (here Hop-Frog sighed), 'and then let us have the benefit of your invention. We want characters – *characters*, man – something novel – out of the way. We are wearied with this everlasting sameness. Come drink! the wine will brighten your wits.'

Hop-Frog endeavoured, as usual, to get up a jest in reply to these advances from the king; but the effort was too much. It happened to be the poor dwarf's birthday, and the command to drink to his 'absent friends' forced the tears to his eyes. Many large, bitter drops fell into the goblet as he took it, humbly, from the hand of the tyrant.

'Ah! ha! ha! ha!' roared the latter, as the dwarf reluctantly drained the beaker. 'See what a glass of good wine can do! Why, your eyes are shining already!'

Poor fellow! his large eyes *gleamed*, rather than shone; for the effect of the wine on his excitable brain was not more powerful than instantaneous. He placed the goblet nervously on the table, and looked round upon the company with a half-insane stare. They all seemed highly amused at the success of the king's '*joke*'.

'And now to business,' said the prime minister, a very fat man.

'Yes,' said the king; 'come Hop-Frog, lend us your assistance. Characters, my fine fellow; we stand in need of characters – all of us – ha! ha! ha!' and as this was seriously meant for a joke, his laugh was chorused by the seven.

Hop-Frog also laughed, although feebly and somewhat vacantly.

'Come, come,' said the king, impatiently, 'have you nothing to suggest?'

'I am endeavouring to think of something *novel*,' replied the dwarf, abstractedly, for he was quite bewildered by the wine.

---

ill humour: bad temper
bumper: glass-full of wine
invention: skill in thinking up ideas
novel: original
endeavoured: tried
instantaneous: immediate
abstractedly: vaguely

COMMENTARY

Everyone is ready for the ball except the king and his ministers. *They* cannot think of what costumes to wear. The two dwarfs are summoned to help. The king is in a 'joking' mood; he enjoys forcing Hop-Frog to drink a lot of wine. It goes straight to his head.

'Endeavouring!' cried the tyrant, fiercely; 'what do you mean by *that*? Ah, I perceive. You are sulky, and want more wine. Here, drink this!' and he poured out another goblet full and offered it to the cripple, who merely gazed at it, gasping for breath.

'Drink, I say!' shouted the monster, 'or by the fiends –'

The dwarf hesitated. The king grew purple with rage. The courtiers smirked. Trippetta, pale as a corpse, advanced to the monarch's seat, and, falling on her knees before him, implored him to spare her friend.

The tyrant regarded her, for some moments, in evident wonder at her audacity. He seemed quite at a loss what to do or say – how most becomingly to express his indignation. At last, without uttering a syllable, he pushed her violently from him, and threw the contents of the brimming goblet in her face.

The poor girl got up as best she could, and, not daring even to sigh, resumed her position at the foot of the table.

There was a dead silence for about a half a minute, during which the falling of a leaf, or of a feather, might have been heard. It was interrupted by a low, but harsh and protracted *grating* sound which seemed to come at once from every corner of the room.

'What – what – *what* are you making that noise for?' demanded the king, turning furiously to the dwarf.

The latter seemed to have recovered in great measure from his intoxication, and looking fixedly but quietly into the tyrant's face, merely ejaculated.

'I – I? How could it have been me?'

'The sound appeared to come from without,' observed one of the courtiers. 'I fancy it was the parrot at the window, whetting his bill upon his cage-wires.'

'True,' replied the monarch, as if much relieved by the suggestion; 'but, on the honour of a knight, I could have sworn that it was the gritting of this vagabond's teeth.'

Hereupon the dwarf laughed (the king was too confirmed a joker to object to any one's laughing), and displayed a set of large, powerful and very repulsive teeth. Moreover, he avowed his perfect willingness to swallow as

COMMENTARY

Hop-Frog is too dazed by drink to help the king, who becomes furious at him. When Trippetta begs the king not to be cruel to her friend, the king flings a glass of wine in her face. A deep silence follows. Then a grating sound is heard – Hop-Frog grinding his teeth.

perceive: understand
fiends: devils
implored: pleaded with
audacity: boldness
indignation: fierce anger
protracted: drawn-out
intoxication: drunken state
ejaculated: exclaimed
without: outside
whetting: sharpening
vagabond: wandering beggar

much wine as desired. The monarch was pacified; and having drained another bumper with no very perceptible ill effect, Hop-Frog entered at once, and with spirit, into the plans for the masquerade.

'I cannot tell what was the association of ideas,' observed he, very tranquilly, and as if he had never tasted wine in his life, 'but *just after* your majesty had struck the girl and thrown the wine in her face – *just after* your majesty had done this, and while the parrot was making that odd noise outside the window, there came into my mind a capital diversion – one of my own country frolics – often enacted among us, at our masquerades: but here it will be new altogether. Unfortunately, however, it requires a company of eight persons, and –'

'Here we *are*!' cried the king, laughing at his acute discovery of the coincidence; 'eight to a fraction – I and my seven ministers. Come! What is the diversion?'

'We call it,' replied the cripple, 'the Eight Chained Ourang-Outangs, and it really is excellent sport if well enacted.'

'*We* will enact it,' remarked the king, drawing himself up, and lowering his eyelids.

'The beauty of the game,' continued Hop-Frog, 'lies in the fright it occasions among the women.'

'Capital!' roared in chorus the monarch and his ministry.

'*I* will help equip you as ourang-outangs,' proceeded the dwarf; 'leave all that to me. The resemblance shall be so striking, that the company of masqueraders will take you for real beasts – and, of course, they will be as much terrified as astonished.'

'O, this is exquisite!' exclaimed the king. 'Hop-Frog, I will make a man of you.'

'The chains are for the purpose of increasing the confusion by their jangling. You are supposed to have escaped, *en masse*, from your keepers. Your majesty cannot conceive the *effect* produced, as a masquerade, by eight chained ourang-outangs, imagined to be real ones by most of the company; and rushing

---

pacified: calmed down
perceptible: noticeable
tranquilly: coolly, quietly
capital diversion: excellent entertainment
Ourang-Outangs: large apes
occasions: causes
conceive: imagine

COMMENTARY
Hop-Frog rapidly sobers up. His manner towards the king changes: he now speaks with calm authority. He suggests that the king and his seven ministers dress up for the masked ball as ourang-outangs. The king is delighted with the idea.

in with savage cries, among the crowd of delicately and gorgeously habited men and women. The *contrast* is inimitable.'

'It *must* be,' said the king: and the council arose hurriedly (as it was growing late), to put in execution the scheme of Hop-Frog.

His mode of equipping the party as ourang-outangs was very simple, but effective enough for his purposes. The animals in question had, at the epoch of my story, very rarely been seen in any part of the civilised world; and as the imitations made by the dwarf were sufficiently beast-like and more than sufficiently hideous, their truthfulness to nature was thus thought to be secured.

PAUSE FOR PLAYBACK:
Now look at the playback questions on page 20 before going on with your reading.

Look out for...
- **the way in which Hop-Frog makes the ourang-outang costumes.**
- **the surprise awaiting the ourang-outangs when they get to the masked ball.**
- **how, by the end of the story, 'the work of vengeance [is] complete'.**

The king and his ministers were first encased in tight-fitting stockinet shirts and drawers. They were then saturated with tar. At this stage in the process, some one of the party suggested feathers; but the suggestion was at once overruled by the dwarf, who soon convinced the eight by ocular demonstration, that the hair of such a brute as the ourang-outang was much more efficiently represented by *flax*. A thick coating of the latter was

COMMENTARY
Hop-Frog explains his scheme further. The ourang-outangs will be chained together, as if they have escaped from their handlers. They will burst in when the masked ball is at its height; everyone will be frightened as well as astonished.

habited: dressed
inimitable: incomparable, unique
in execution: into practice
epoch: date
drawers: tights
by ocular demonstration: by showing them

accordingly plastered upon the coating of tar. A long chain was now procured. First, it was passed about the waist of the king, *and tied*; then about another of the party, and also tied; then about all successively, in the same manner. When this chaining arrangement was complete, and the party stood as far apart from each other as possible, they formed a circle; and to make all things appear natural, Hop-Frog passed the residue of the chain, in two diameters, at right angles, across the circle, after the fashion adopted, at the present day, by those who capture Chimpanzees, or other large apes, in Borneo.

The grand saloon, in which the masquerade was to take place, was a circular room, very lofty, and receiving the light of the sun only through a single window at top. At night (the season for which the apartment was especially designed), it was illuminated principally by a large chandelier, depending by a chain from the centre of the skylight, and lowered, or elevated, by means of a counterbalance as usual; but (in order not to look unsightly) this latter passed outside the cupola and over the roof.

The arrangements of the room had been left to Trippetta's superintendance: but, in some particulars, it seems, she had been guided by the calmer judgement of her friend the dwarf. At his suggestion it was that, on this occasion, the chandelier was removed. Its waxen drippings (which, in weather so warm, it was quite impossible to prevent), would have been seriously detrimental to the rich dresses of the guests, who, on account of the crowded state of the saloon, could not *all* be expected to keep from out its centre – that is to say, from under the chandelier. Additional sconces were set in various parts of the hall, out of the way; and a flambeau, emitting sweet odour, was placed in the right hand of each of the Caryatides that stood against the wall – some fifty or sixty altogether.

The eight ourang-outangs, taking Hop-Frog's advice, waited patiently until midnight (when the room was thoroughly filled with masqueraders) before making their appearance. No sooner had the clock ceased striking, however, than they rushed, or rather rolled in, all together – for the impediment of their chains caused most of the party to fall, and all to stumble as they entered.

residue: remainder
grand saloon: finest large hall
depending by: hanging from
elevated: raised
cupola: dome in the ceiling
drippings: i.e. from the chandelier's candles
detrimental: damaging
sconces: candle-holders
flambeau: flaming torch
Caryatides: stone statues of Greek women
impediment: obstruction

COMMENTARY
Preparations begin. Hop-Frog provides the king and his ministers with costumes that make them look like hairy beasts. Then all eight are tied together. Trippetta is in charge of the ball-room, where a huge chandelier normally hangs from a chain high in the ceiling.

The excitement among the masqueraders was prodigious, and filled the heart of the king with glee. As had been anticipated, there were not a few of the guests who supposed the ferocious-looking creatures to be beasts of *some* kind in reality, if not precisely ourang-outangs. Many of the women swooned with affright, and had not the king taken precaution to exclude all weapons from the saloon, his party might soon have expiated their frolic in their blood. As it was, a general rush was made for the doors; but the king had ordered them to be locked immediately upon his entrance; and, at the dwarf's suggestion, the keys were deposited with *him*.

While the tumult was at its height, and each masquerader attentive only to his own safety – (for, in fact, there was much *real* danger from the pressure of the excited crowd) – the chain by which the chandelier ordinarily hung, and which had been drawn up on its removal, might have been seen very gradually to descend, until its hooked extremity came within three feet of the floor.

Soon after this, the king and his seven friends, having reeled about the hall in all directions, found themselves, at length, in its centre, and, of course, in immediate contact with the chain. While they were thus situated, the dwarf, who had followed closely at their heels, inciting them to keep up the commotion, took hold of their own chain at the intersection of the two portions which crossed the circle diametrically and at right angles. Here, with the rapidity of thought, he inserted the hook from which the chandelier had been wont to depend; and, in an instant, by some unseen agency, the chandelier-chain was drawn so far upward as to take the hook out of reach, and, as an inevitable consequence, to drag the ourang-outangs together in close connection, and face to face.

The masqueraders, by this time, had recovered, in some measure, from their alarm; and beginning to regard the whole matter as a well-contrived pleasantry, set up a loud shout of laughter at the predicament of the apes.

'Leave them to *me*!' now screamed Hop-Frog, his shrill voice making itself easily heard through all the din. 'Leave them to *me*. I fancy *I* know them. If I can only get a good look at them, I can soon tell who they are.'

COMMENTARY

The masked ball starts. The chandelier has been removed from the ceiling: only its chain remains. At midnight, the eight ourang-outangs rush in. They cause a tremendous sensation. No one notices the chain, with a hook on its lower end, descending to the floor.

expiated: paid for
inciting: urging
inserted: attached
had been wont to depend: usually hung
well-contrived pleasantry: cleverly planned game

Here, scrambling over the heads of the crowd, he managed to get to the wall; when, seizing a flambeau from one of the Caryatides, he returned, as he went, to the centre of the room – leaped, with the agility of a monkey, upon the king's head – and thence clambered a few feet up the chain – holding down the torch to examine the group of ourang-outangs, and still screaming, '*I* shall soon find out who they are!'

And now, while the whole assembly (the apes included) were convulsed with laughter, the jester suddenly uttered a shrill whistle; when the chain flew violently up for about thirty feet – dragging with it the dismayed and struggling ourang-outangs, and leaving them suspended in mid-air between the sky-light and the floor. Hop-Frog, clinging to the chain as it rose, still maintained his relative position in respect to the eight maskers, and still (as if nothing were the matter) continued to thrust his torch down towards them, as though endeavouring to discover who they were.

So thoroughly astonished were the whole company at this ascent, that a dead silence, of about a minute's duration, ensued. It was broken by just such a low, harsh, *grating* sound, as had before attracted the attention of the king and his councillors, when the former threw the wine in the face of Trippetta. But, on the present occasion, there could be no question as to *whence* the sound issued. It came from the fang-like teeth of the dwarf, who ground them and gnashed them as he foamed at the mouth, and glared, with an expression of maniacal rage, into the upturned countenances of the king and his seven companions.

'Ah, ha!' said at length the infuriated jester. 'Ah ha! I begin to see who these people *are*, now!' Here, pretending to scrutinize the king more closely, he held the flambeau to the flaxen coat which enveloped him, and which instantly burst into a sheet of vivid flame. In less than half a minute the whole eight ourang-outangs were blazing fiercely, amid the shrieks of the multitude who gazed at them from below, horror-stricken, and without the power to render them the slightest assistance.

At length the flames, suddenly increasing in virulence, forced the jester to

relative: i.e. close to them
duration: length
whence: from where
issued: came
maniacal: wild, insane
countenances: faces
scrutinize: examine
virulence: strength

COMMENTARY
Rapidly, Hop-Frog hooks the group of ourang-outangs, still linked together, to the chain. He whistles. They are pulled upwards and hang helpless in mid-air. Hop-Frog, clinging to the chain above their heads, 'inspects' them by the light of a flaming torch and then sets them alight.

climb higher up the chain, to be out of their reach; and, as he made this movement, the crowd again sank, for a brief instant, into silence. The dwarf seized his opportunity, and once more spoke:

'I now see *distinctly*,' he said 'what manner of people these maskers are. They are a great king and his seven privy-councillors – a king who does not scruple to strike a defenceless girl, and his seven councillors who abet him in the outrage. As for myself, I am simply Hop-Frog, the jester – and *this is my last jest.*'

Owing to the combustibility of both the flax and the tar to which it adhered, the dwarf had scarcely made an end of his brief speech before the work of vengeance was complete. The eight corpses swung in their chains, a fetid, blackened, hideous, and indistinguishable mass. The cripple hurled his torch at them, clambered leisurely to the ceiling, and disappeared through the sky-light.

It is supposed that Trippetta, stationed on the roof of the saloon, had been the accomplice of her friend in his fiery revenge, and that, together, they effected their escape to their own country: for neither was seen again.

PAUSE FOR PLAYBACK:
Now look at the playback questions on page 20.

COMMENTARY

Hop-Frog then tells everyone present about the king's cruel treatment of Trippetta. The king and his ministers burn to death.

Trippetta is waiting for her friend on the roof. It is she who has operated the chain. Hop-Frog climbs through the sky-light to join her, and the two dwarfs return to their homeland.

does not scruple: cares nothing; has no conscience about
combustibility: readiness to burn
fetid: stinking
stationed: positioned
effected: made

Study guide

PLAYBACK QUESTIONS

PAGES 9 TO 15:

- ➤ What picture do you have of the king's appearance? Up to now, what are your impressions of his character?
- ➤ What do Hop-Frog and Trippetta have in common? In what ways do they *differ*?
- ➤ At what point, exactly, does Hop-Frog become sober after the wine first goes to his head? Why does he 'sober up' so quickly, do you think?
- ➤ What impression do you imagine the king and his ministers will make at the masked ball in their ourang-outang costumes?

Now return to reading the story on page 15

PAGES 15 TO 19:

- ➤ On what grounds does Hop-Frog persuade the king to remove the chandelier from the ballroom? What are his *real* reasons for wanting it out of the way?
- ➤ Re-read the passage where Hop-Frog 'hooks up' the king and his ministers. How does he manage it, exactly? Why does he let out a 'shrill whistle' afterwards?
- ➤ Do you think the king and his ministers deserve their fate? Why, or why not?
- ➤ What do you imagine might happen to Hop-Frog and Trippetta after the end of the story?

Reviewing the whole story: suggested activities

1 The Hop-Frog video

A film company is bringing out a number of short videos, *Tales of the Grotesque*. *Hop-Frog* is to be the first in the series.

a **As a class**, discuss how effective the story is likely to be in film form. Amongst other things, you should consider:

- does the story-line lend itself well to being filmed? If you were the director, would you make any changes to the plot as Poe wrote it?

- how much 'visual appeal' would the story have on film? Think about the physical appearance of the main characters, the setting for the main events, and the climax of the story.

- what feelings you would want to arouse in the viewer.

b **With a partner**, you have the job of publicising the *Hop-Frog* video. Plan and produce:

- a suitable advertising poster to be distributed to video stores.

- a 50 to 75 word 'blurb' to be printed on the back of the video box. (This should arouse people's interest without giving away too much.)

c Recently released video films are reviewed in magazines and other printed media.

In a group, collect a number of reviews of new videos. Read them carefully. Talk about the information they give and the style(s) in which they are written.

d **By yourself**, plan and write a review of the video-version of *Hop-Frog* which was released last week. You should include comments on:

- the plot and the main characters.

- the film's technical (and/or special) effects.

- how you were made to feel as you watched.

- how successful you think the film was, and why you would (or would not) recommend it.

- anything else you consider important.

2 | Hop-Frog's grievances

Hop-Frog has strong reasons for feeling that he has been treated badly by life in general and by the king in particular.

a   **In a group**, re-read the story *aloud* from the beginning to page 13. Stop at the paragraph ending 'threw the contents of the brimming goblet in her face'.

Divide up this extract so that you each read aloud twice. Before you begin, check the glossary for the meanings of any difficult words which come in 'your' sections.

b   Talk about the grievances Hop-Frog has and the reasons for them. Each of you should note down what you decide by making a chart, like this:

Reasons for grievance	Evidence	Extent
1. H-F's nickname is cruel: makes fun of his deformity	'It was conferred upon him by general consent of the seven courtiers' (page 10)	?
2.		

Fill in the 'Extent' column by using a numbering system 1 to 5, where 1 = 'a slight grievance' and 5 = 'a very deep grievance'. You should make between six and nine entries on your chart.

c   After Hop-Frog's escape at the end of the story, a letter is found in his room addressed to 'My enemies'. In it he describes fully all the grievances which led him to take revenge on the king and his ministers. The letter refers to Hop-Frog's life in the past as well as to the time covered by the story.

Think not only about what Hop-Frog will say but also about the way in which he will say it. He is an educated man who can express himself intelligently. What *tone* will he use? Will he, for instance, come over as spiteful and twisted, or as calm and reasonable? **By yourself**, write Hop-Frog's letter.

3 | Plotting revenge

'It is supposed that Trippetta, stationed on the roof of the saloon, had been the accomplice of her friend in his fiery revenge' (page 19).

a   **With a partner**, put yourselves in the place of Hop-Frog and Trippetta. Referring back to the story, plot in detail the revenge you are going to take during the masquerade.

b   Speak to each other in role. As you talk, use a large sheet of paper to make lists, notes, diagrams etc. so that you can be *certain* everything will work out as you wish – including your escape at the end.

c   You will need to re-read the story from pages 14 to 19 in order to come up with a foolproof plan. It will not be easy. For instance:

   ● how will you ensure that the king and courtiers never suspect they are being tricked to their deaths?

   ● how will Hop-Frog convince the king that the chandelier in the saloon must be removed?

   ● how will Trippetta get herself onto the roof and know exactly when to operate the chain?

d   When you are satisfied you have covered everything, **join up with another pair**. Compare your 'revenge plots'. Award each other a mark out of ten for the thoroughness, practicality and ingenuity of the plans you have made.

4 | Only joking!

In *Hop-Frog*, the king is the victim of his own liking for practical jokes.

a   **As a class**, talk about practical jokes that *you* have played in the past – and/or about practical jokes that have been played on you. Did any of them go terribly wrong? Did they lead to trouble?

b   **By yourself**, write your own real or imagined story about a 'joke' which *either* succeeded *or* which seriously backfired. Try to bring out clearly:

   ● the motives of the 'joker'.

   ● how the victim was 'set up'.

   ● the feelings of the 'joker' both before and after the event.

   ● how the victim reacted and what his/her other feelings were afterwards.

5 Horror struck

Edgar Allan Poe is often described as 'the father of the horror story'. Many modern-day writers have been influenced by him. Stephen King, for instance, names *Hop-Frog* as his favourite Poe short story.

The purpose of this activity is to examine what it is, exactly, that goes to make a horror story, and to decide whether *Hop-Frog* is a good one.

a   **In a group**, talk about horror stories, films and videos that you have read or seen.

What do they have in common? What makes them effective?

As you talk, each make a spider-diagram headed '***Common elements in horror stories***', like this:

Give your spider-diagram as many 'legs' as there are different points to make.

b   Use your findings to take part in a **class discussion** about horror stories. Make a full class-list of all the common elements you agree about.

c   **As a class**, take each item on your list and consider it in relation to *Hop-Frog*. Highlight the elements that apply to Poe's story. Then, for each of them, try to agree how well they are used by the author. To show what you think, give each element a mark out of ten, according to the following key:

9 or 10	Excellent
7 or 8	Good
5 or 6	Just average
3 or 4	Poor
1 or 2	Very poor

d **With a partner**, draw on all the work you have done so far to plan a written account of the 'horror' (or 'horrific') elements in *Hop-Frog*.

The purpose of your writing is two-fold: (i) to identify and describe what the horrific elements in the story are, and (ii) to state how effective you find them.

How to plan your writing

- Consider every element you have noted down on your spider-diagram. Take them in the order you wish. For each, find at least one example from the story and make a note of *quotations* you can use to illustrate it.

- Referring back to **c** above, make notes on the *effectiveness* of each element. At this stage, you must be prepared to put forward clear reasons for whatever judgements you make. It may prove helpful to make comparisons between *Hop-Frog* and other horror stories you know – either in this volume or from your wider reading.

- Consider how you are going to *paragraph* your writing. This involves deciding on (i) the order in which you will make your points, (ii) how one paragraph will lead naturally on to the next, and (iii) what to include in your introductory and concluding paragraphs.

e When you have completed your plan, show it to your teacher for comment. Make any changes you consider necessary in the light of the feedback you get. If you are unsure about how to use and/or set out quotations, ask.

f **By yourself**, use your notes to write a detailed essay on the following title:

'What elements in *Hop-Frog* make it a classic horror story? Say, with reasons supported by quotation, how effective you consider it to be.'

At the end of the essay, write in note-form a comment to your teacher saying what you think you have done *well* in the essay and what you think you need further help with when you write in this way about literature.

THE TELL-TALE HEART

Look out for…
- **the kind of man the story-teller (or 'narrator') seems to be.**
- **what the tell-tale heart actually is, and why it plays an important part in the story.**

True! – nervous – very, very dreadfully nervous I had been and am; but why *will* you say that I am mad? The disease had sharpened my senses – not destroyed – not dulled them. Above all was the sense of hearing acute. I heard all things in the heaven and in the earth. I heard many things in hell. How, then, am I mad? Hearken! and observe how healthily – how calmly I can tell you the whole story.

It is impossible to say how first the idea entered my brain: but once conceived, it haunted me day and night. Object there was none. Passion there was none. I loved the old man. He had never wronged me. He had never given me insult. For his gold I had no desire. I think it was his eye! yes, it was this! One of his eyes resembled that of a vulture – a pale blue eye, with a film over it. Whenever it fell upon me, my blood ran cold; and so by degrees – very gradually – I made up my mind to take the life of the old man, and thus rid myself of the eye for ever.

Now this is the point. You fancy me mad. Madmen know nothing. But you should have seen *me*. You should have seen how wisely I proceeded – with what caution – with what foresight – with what dissimulation I went to work! I was never kinder to the old man than during the whole week before I killed him.

COMMENTARY
The narrator has murdered an old man. He is telling the story of how and why he did it – in order to show, he claims, that he was not mad at the time.

Hearken!: Listen carefully!
conceived: fixed in my mind
Object: Purpose (such as doing it for money)
Passion: Strong feeling (such as hatred)
fancy: imagine
dissimulation: cunning deceit

And every night, about midnight, I turned the latch of his door and opened it – oh so gently! And then, when I had made an opening sufficient for my head, I put in a dark lantern, all closed, closed, so that no light shone out, and then I thrust in my head. Oh, you would have laughed to see how cunningly I thrust it in! I moved it slowly – very, very slowly, so that I might not disturb the old man's sleep. It took me an hour to place my whole head within the opening so far that I could see him as he lay upon his bed. Ha! – would a madman have been so wise as this? And then, when my head was well in the room, I undid the lantern cautiously – oh, so cautiously – cautiously (for the hinges creaked) – I undid it just so much that a single thin ray fell upon the vulture eye. And this I did for seven long nights – every night just at midnight – but I found the eye always closed; and so it was impossible to do the work; for it was not the old man who vexed me, but his Evil Eye. And every morning, when the day broke, I went boldly into the chamber, and spoke courageously to him, calling him by name in a hearty tone, and inquiring how he had passed the night. So you see he would have been a very profound old man, indeed, to suspect that every night, just at twelve, I looked in upon him while he slept.

Upon the eighth night I was more than usually cautious in opening the door. A watch's minute hand moves more quickly than did mine. Never, before that night, had I *felt* the extent of my own powers – of my sagacity. I could scarcely contain my feelings of triumph. To think that there I was, opening the door, little by little, and he not even to dream of my secret deeds or thoughts. I fairly chuckled at the idea; and perhaps he heard me; for he moved on the bed suddenly, as if startled. Now you may think that I drew back – but no. His room was black as pitch with the thick darkness (for the shutters were close fastened, through fear of robbers), and so I knew that he could not see the opening of the door, and I kept pushing it on steadily, steadily.

I had my head in, and was about to open the lantern, when my thumb slipped upon the tin fastening, and the old man sprang up in the bed, crying out – 'Who's there?'

---

dark lantern: a lantern that can have its
   light covered
vexed: upset, annoyed
profound: clever
sagacity: intelligence, slyness

COMMENTARY
Every night for a week, on the stroke of twelve, the murderer visits the old man while he is sleeping. He is obsessed by his victim's Evil Eye. On his eighth midnight visit to the old man's room, the murderer wakes him with an accidental noise.

I kept quite still and said nothing. For a whole hour I did not move a muscle, and in the meantime I did not hear him lie down. He was still sitting up in the bed, listening – just as I have done, night after night, hearkening to the death-watches in the wall.

Presently, I heard a slight groan, and I knew it was the groan of mortal terror. It was not a groan of pain or of grief – oh, no! – it was the low stifled sound that arises from the bottom of the soul when overcharged with awe. I knew the sound well. Many a time, just at midnight, when all the world slept, it has welled up from my own bosom, deepening, with its dreadful echo, the terrors that distracted me. I say I knew it well. I knew what the old man felt, and pitied him, although I chuckled at heart. I knew that he had been lying awake ever since the first slight noise, when he had turned in the bed. His fears had been ever since growing upon him. He had been trying to fancy them causeless, but could not. He had been saying to himself – 'It is nothing but the wind in the chimney – it is only a mouse crossing the floor', or 'it is merely a cricket which has made a single chirp'. Yes, he had been trying to comfort himself with all these suppositions: but he had found all in vain. *All in vain*; because Death, in approaching him, had stalked with his black shadow before him, and enveloped the victim. And it was the mournful influence of the unperceived shadow that caused him to feel – although he neither saw nor heard – to *feel* the presence of my head within the room.

When I had waited a long time, very patiently, without hearing him lie down, I resolved to open a little – a very, very little crevice in the lantern. So I opened it – you cannot imagine how stealthily, stealthily – until at length, a single dim ray, like the thread of the spider, shot from out the crevice and fell upon the vulture eye.

It was open – wide, wide open – and I grew furious as I gazed upon it.

I saw it with perfect distinctness – all a dull blue, with a hideous veil over it that chilled the very marrow in my bones; but I could see nothing else of the old man's face or person: for I had directed the ray, as if by instinct, precisely upon the damned spot.

COMMENTARY

The murderer watches, with a mixture of pity and pleasure, his victim's terror. After an hour, he shines his lantern onto the old man's eye.

death-watches: death-watch beetles, which make a ticking sound
overcharged with awe: overcome with fear
distracted me: drove me half-mad
unperceived shadow: unseen ghost of Death
distinctness: clarity

And now – have I not told you that what you mistake for madness is but over-acuteness of the senses? – now, I say, there came to my ears a low, dull, quick sound, such as a watch makes when enveloped in cotton. I knew *that* sound well, too. It was the beating of the old man's heart. It increased my fury, as the beating of a drum stimulates the soldier into courage.

But even yet I refrained and kept still. I scarcely breathed. I held the lantern motionless. I tried how steadily I could maintain the ray upon the eye. Meantime, the hellish tattoo of the heart increased. It grew quicker and quicker, and louder and louder every instant. The old man's terror *must* have been extreme! It grew louder, I say, louder every moment – do you mark me well? I have told you that I am nervous: so I am. And now at the dead hour of the night, amid the dreadful silence of that old house, so strange a noise as this excited me to uncontrollable terror. Yet, for some minutes longer I refrained and stood still. But the beating grew louder, louder! I thought the heart must burst. And now a new anxiety seized me – the sound would be heard by a neighbour! The old man's hour had come! With a loud yell, I threw open the lantern and leaped into the room. He shrieked once – once only. In an instant I dragged him to the floor, and pulled the heavy bed over him. I then smiled gaily, to find the deed so far done. But, for many minutes, the heart beat on with a muffled sound. This, however, did not vex me; it would not be heard through the wall. At length it ceased. The old man was dead. I removed the bed and examined the corpse. Yes, he was stone, stone dead. I placed my hand upon the heart and held it there many minutes. There was no pulsation. He was stone dead. His eye would trouble me no more.

If still you think me mad, you will think so no longer when I describe the wise precautions I took for the concealment of the body. The night waned, and I worked hastily, but in silence. First of all I dismembered the corpse. I cut off the head and the arms and the legs.

I then took up three planks from the flooring of the chamber, and deposited all beneath the scantlings. I then replaced the boards so cleverly, so cunningly, that no human eye – not even *his* – could have detected anything wrong. There

---

but over-acuteness of the senses: only a case
   of me being too sensitive to sound,
   sight, touch, etc.
refrained: held back
tried: i.e. tried to find out
mark me: attend to what I say
excited me: aroused me
lantern: i.e. the lantern's shutter
waned: drew on towards morning
scantlings: supporting beams, joists

COMMENTARY

The murderer can hear the old man's heart beating with terror. Fearing someone else will hear it through the wall, he drags the old man under the bed. After a while, the heart stops. The murderer chops up and hides his victim's body.

was nothing to wash out – no stain of any kind – no blood-spot whatever. I had been too wary for that. A tub had caught all – ha! ha!

When I had made an end of these labours, it was four o'clock – still dark as midnight. As the bell sounded the hour, there came a knocking at the street door. I went down to open it with a light heart, – for what had I *now* to fear? There entered three men, who introduced themselves, with perfect suavity, as officers of the police. A shriek had been heard by a neighbour during the night; suspicion of foul play had been aroused; information had been lodged at the police office, and they (the officers) had been deputed to search the premises.

I smiled – for *what* had I to fear? I bade the gentlemen welcome. The shriek, I said, was my own in a dream. The old man, I mentioned, was absent in the country. I took my visitors all over the house. I bade them search – search *well*. I led them, at length, to *his* chamber. I showed them his treasures, secure, undisturbed. In the enthusiasm of my confidence, I brought chairs into the room, and desired them *here* to rest from their fatigues, while I myself, in the wild audacity of my perfect triumph, placed my own seat upon the very spot beneath which reposed the corpse of the victim.

The officers were satisfied. My *manner* had convinced them. I was singularly at ease. They sat, and while I answered cheerily, they chatted of familiar things. But, ere long, I felt myself getting pale and wished them gone. My head ached, and I fancied a ringing in my ears: but still they sat and chatted. The ringing became more distinct: – it continued and became more distinct: I talked more freely to get rid of the feeling: but it continued and gained definitiveness – until, at length, I found that the noise was *not* within my ears.

No doubt I now grew *very* pale; – but I talked more fluently, and with a heightened voice. Yet the sound increased – and what could I do? It was a *low, dull, quick sound – much such a sound as a watch makes when enveloped in cotton.* I gasped for breath – and yet the officers heard it not. I talked more quickly – more vehemently; but the noise steadily increased. I arose and argued about trifles, in a high key with violent gesticulations; but the noise steadily

COMMENTARY

Police officers arrive: a scream from the house has been reported. The murderer, confident that he has nothing to fear, cooperates with them fully in their search. After a while, he hears a sound he knows well: the beating of a terrified heart.

made an end: finished
suavity: politeness
their fatigues: their tiring work
audacity: boldness
singularly: remarkably
ere: before
vehemently: loudly, emotionally
trifles: trivial things
gesticulations: arm-waving

increased. Why *would* they not be gone? I paced the floor to and fro with heavy strides, as if excited to fury by the observations of the men – but the noise steadily increased. Oh God! what *could* I do? I foamed – I raved – I swore! I swung the chair upon which I had been sitting, and grated it upon the boards, but the noise arose over all and continually increased. It grew louder – louder – *louder*! And still the men chatted pleasantly, and smiled. Was it possible they heard not? Almighty God! – no, no! They heard! – they suspected – they knew! – they were making a mockery of my horror! – this I thought, and this I think. But anything was better than this agony! Anything was more tolerable than this derision! I could bear those hypocritical smiles no longer! I felt that I must scream or die! and now – again! – hark! louder! louder! louder! *louder*!

'Villains!' I shrieked, 'dissemble no more! I admit the deed! – tear up the planks! – here, here! – it is the beating of his hideous heart!'

PAUSE FOR PLAYBACK:
Now look at the playback questions on page 33.

---

tolerable: bearable
derision: ridicule, mockery
dissemble no more!: stop pretending!

COMMENTARY
The murderer is convinced that the officers can hear the beating heart too. Unable to bear it any longer, he confesses his crime.

Study guide

PAGES 27 TO 32:

➤ Throughout the story, the narrator is speaking to someone. Who do you think it might be? Why?

➤ Why does the narrator seem to have such a strong grudge against the old man? Does it seem to you to be a justifiable one?

➤ 'Oh, you would have laughed to see how cunningly I thrust it [i.e. the lantern] in!' (page 28). Would *you* have laughed?

➤ As he sets about terrifying the old man, the narrator has a mixture of feelings. What are they? How do you explain them?

* * * * *

➤ How do you think the old man dies, exactly?

➤ The narrator says that what he does with the dead body is a 'wise precaution' (page 30). How would *you* describe it?

➤ 'The officers were satisfied' (page 31). If you had been one of the police officers who visited the house, would *you* have been 'satisfied' of the narrator's innocence? Why, or why not?

➤ In the end, the narrator confesses to murdering the old man. What is his explanation of why he does so? Is yours the same?

REVIEWING THE WHOLE STORY: SUGGESTED ACTIVITIES

1 'Why *will* you say that I am mad?'

In *The Tell-Tale Heart*, the murderer repeatedly denies being mad. This activity asks you to decide whether he really is.

a **With a partner**, find evidence from the first half of the story to show that the murderer:

- has none of the 'normal' motives for killing someone.
- thoroughly enjoys terrorising the old man.
- feels a gleeful sense of power in the week leading up to the old man's death.
- has no conscience after he carries out the murder.

Note down all the evidence you find, fully and in detail.

b **As a class**, look closely at the second half of the story describing what happens after the murder. What does it tell you about the murderer's state of mind? Focus in particular on:

- why the murderer thinks he has been extremely clever.
- his confidence that he will never be caught.
- the reason why 'I foamed, I raved, I swore'.
- the way in which the truth comes out.

Make detailed notes on what you decide.

c **In a group**, role-play an interview between several psychiatrists and the murderer, following his arrest. The psychiatrists are questioning him to see whether he should be executed for his crime, or put in a mental hospital for life on the grounds of 'diminished responsibility' – that is, he was not in control of his actions because he was mentally disturbed.

Decide who will play the part of the murderer. He must answer in character throughout the interview. The psychiatrists should prepare a list of between four and six questions to put to him, in order to make what sense they can of his behaviour.

d **By yourself**, draw on all the work you have done during this activity to plan and write a 'psychiatrist's report' on the murderer. In it you should say:

- what evidence there is that he was not in his right mind.

- what evidence there is that he deliberately set out to murder the old man – and that he took pleasure in doing it.

- what your recommendations are about what should be done to him.

You should write your report in a formal style and in a clearly argued way. Avoid using slang; write in Standard English throughout.

2 | 'My *manner* had convinced them'

Before he confesses at the end of the story, the murderer is certain that he has proved his innocence to the police. In fact, without realising it he has given them plenty of reasons to suspect him very strongly.

Explore the text to work out what these reasons are:

a **By yourself**, re-read the part of the story running from 'I smiled – for *what* had I to fear?' (page 31) to 'Oh God! What *could* I do?' (page 32).

b **With a partner**, put yourself in the place of two of the police officers. Using a large sheet of paper, make entries in your Notebook under the heading 'Observations', like this:

Investigation of: Reported loud scream – house in residential area

Time of arrival: 4 a.m.

Person interviewed: Male resident alone in house (lodger?)

Observations: Male resident's behaviour suspicious – e.g.:

1 Fully dressed and wide awake at 4 a.m.
2 First reaction to police arrival: a satisfied smile
3

You could find up to *ten* examples of 'suspicious' behaviour.

c **Join up with another pair**. Compare notes. Stay in your role as police officers and explain fully to each other *why* you have made the entries you have – e.g.: 'When he opened the door, he didn't show any surprise at seeing us. We thought it was strange when he smiled: people usually look shocked and worried when the police call, especially in the middle of the night.'

d   Use your notes to take part in a **class discussion** about how the murderer virtually gives himself away before he confesses. Finish off by discussing whether you would have had enough evidence to arrest him 'on suspicion' if he had *not* confessed.

3   Speak-write

The Tell-Tale Heart is a 'spoken story'. All the way through, the murderer speaks to an unnamed listener in the first person – that is, he uses 'I' – rather than in the third person ('**He** leaped through the bedroom window. **She** screamed').

The purpose of this activity is (i) to explore why Poe wrote *The Tell-Tale Heart* in the way he did, and (ii) to decide what impression the first-person style of the story makes on the reader.

a   **With a partner**, re-read *aloud* the opening two paragraphs of the story. Take one paragraph each.

Although it is written down, the story sounds more like speech – nowhere more so than in these paragraphs. Agree on at least *three* reasons why they read more like speech than normal writing.

b   **By yourself**, read the passage below. It is a third-person version of the story's first paragraph.

> The man agreed that what had been said to him was true. He *was* a highly nervous person. However, he argued strongly that this was no reason for calling him mad. His illness, he claimed, had not left him insane; on the contrary, it had sharpened up his senses, particularly his hearing. He could hear more than other people, including things in his own mind. He offered to tell his whole story in order to prove that he was perfectly normal, healthy and calm.

Now make notes in answer to the following questions.

- Which version do you find more interesting to read – and why?
- What differences are there between the *sentences* in these two versions?
- Which version gives you a better impression of the man's character? Why?
- What differences can you find in the *punctuation* of the two versions?

c   Use your notes to take part in a **class discussion** about the differences between the style of Poe's first paragraph and the version above. Talk about which one is, in your opinion, the more effective piece of writing. Make sure you give clear reasons for what you say.

d   **With a partner**, look again at the last two paragraphs of the story. First
read them to yourself. Then read them aloud, taking the sentences turn-
by-turn. Put as much expression into your reading as possible.

e   **By yourself**, imagine that the murderer's 'spoken story' goes on to
describe the night before his execution. He is in the condemned cell. Using
the same style as that in *The Tell-Tale Heart*, write down the murderer's
thoughts and feelings in about 300 words.

4   'You're nicked!'

In *The Tell-Tale Heart*, the murderer is certain that he can – and does – fool the
police officers. It happens that, even without his confession, he is wrong.

a   **By yourself**, plan, draft and write an imagined story in which a criminal
wrongly believes that s/he has 'got away it'. The crime is up to you to
decide, except that it must *not* be a murder.

In planning, use the following question-guidelines to help you:

-   How are you going to describe the crime? Will the criminal tell his/her
    own story?

-   What 'mistakes' does the criminal make without realising it?

-   How do the police come to be involved?

-   How and why do the police 'see through' the criminal's alibi or attempt
    to cover things up? (You need to be very skilful in the way you write
    this.)

-   What happens to the criminal in the end?

b   When you have drafted the story, show it to your teacher for comment.
Listen carefully to any advice you are given. Then write it up in 'best'
form.

c   **With a partner**, take it in turns to read your stories aloud to each other.
Express an honest opinion about what you hear. You might like to give
your partner's story a grade, or mark out of ten, for the following:

-   How realistic is the way in which the crime is described?

-   Are the criminal's mistakes over-obvious or believable?

-   How clever do the police have to be in solving the crime?

-   Does the story have an effective 'shape' (or structure) and is it
    interestingly told?

THE MASQUE OF THE RED DEATH

Look out for...
- **the way in which Prince Prospero tries to escape from the plague: does he succeed?**
- **the mysterious figure who appears at the masked ball: who is he?**
- **the way Poe builds up an atmosphere of horror: is it effective?**

The 'Red Death' had long devastated the country. No pestilence had ever been so fatal, or so hideous. Blood was its Avatar and its seal – the redness and the horror of blood. There were sharp pains, and sudden dizziness, and then profuse bleeding at the pores, with dissolution. The scarlet stains upon the body and especially upon the face of the victim, were the pest ban which shut him out from the aid and from the sympathy of his fellow-men. And the whole seizure, progress, and termination of the disease, were the incidents of half an hour.

But the Prince Prospero was happy and dauntless and sagacious. When his dominions were half depopulated, he summoned to his presence a thousand hale and light-hearted friends from among the knights and dames of his court, and with these retired to the deep seclusion of one of his castellated abbeys. This was an extensive and magnificent structure, the creation of the prince's own eccentric yet august taste. A strong and lofty wall girdled it in. This wall had gates of iron. The courtiers, having entered, brought furnaces and massy hammers and welded the bolts. They resolved to leave means neither of ingress nor egress to the sudden impulses of despair or of frenzy from within.

COMMENTARY

A terrible plague has already wiped out half the population of Prince Prospero's kingdom. To prevent it reaching him, he walls himself up inside a fortified abbey together with a thousand knights and ladies.

pestilence: plague
Avatar: the form it took
dissolution: rapid decay of the body
termination: the end (i.e. death)
dauntless: not easily frightened
sagacious: clever, shrewd
hale: healthy
august: elegant
ingress nor egress: a way in nor a way out

The abbey was amply provisioned. With such precautions the courtiers might bid defiance to contagion. The external world could take care of itself. In the meantime it was folly to grieve, or to think. The prince had provided all the appliances of pleasure. There were buffoons, there were improvisatori, there were ballet-dancers, there were musicians, there was Beauty, there was wine. All these and security were within. Without was the 'Red Death'.

It was toward the close of the fifth or sixth month of his seclusion, and while the pestilence raged most furiously abroad, that the Prince Prospero entertained his thousand friends at a masked ball of the most unusual magnificence.

It was a voluptuous scene, that masquerade. But first let me tell of the rooms in which it was held. These were seven – an imperial suite. In many palaces, however, such suites form a long and straight vista, while the folding doors slide back nearly to the walls on either hand, so that the view of the whole extent is scarcely impeded. Here the case was very different; as might have been expected from the duke's love of the bizarre. The apartments were so irregularly disposed that the vision embraced but little more than one at a time. There was a sharp turn at every twenty or thirty yards, and at each turn a novel effect. To the right and left, in the middle of each wall, a tall and narrow Gothic window looked out upon a closed corridor which pursued the windings of the suite. These windows were of stained glass whose colour varied in accordance with the prevailing hue of the decorations of the chamber into which it opened. That at the eastern extremity was hung, for example, in blue – and vividly blue were its windows. The second chamber was purple in its ornaments and tapestries, and here the panes were purple. The third was green throughout, and so were the casements. The fourth was furnished and lighted with orange – the fifth with white – the sixth with violet. The seventh apartment was closely shrouded in black velvet tapestries that hung all over the ceiling and down the walls, falling in heavy folds upon a carpet of the same material and hue. But in this chamber only, the colour of the windows failed to correspond with the decorations. The panes here were scarlet – a deep blood

---

buffoons: clowns, jesters
improvisatori: actors
Without: Outside
voluptuous: gorgeous, colourful
bizarre: fantastical
irregularly disposed: not built symmetrically
novel effect: different view
prevailing hue: dominant colour

COMMENTARY

Prince Prospero provides more than enough food, drink and entertainment to keep his guests happy and their minds off the plague.

The rooms where a masked ball is to be held are unusual. They are all at different angles. Each one is decorated throughout in its own single vivid colour, which is matched by the stained glass of the window panes.

colour. Now in not one of the seven apartments was there any lamp or candelabrum, amid the profusion of golden ornaments that lay scattered to and fro or depended from the roof. There was no light of any kind emanating from lamp or candle within the suite of chambers. But in the corridors that followed the suite there stood, opposite to each window, a heavy tripod, bearing a brazier of fire that projected its rays through the tinted glass and so glaringly illuminated the room. And thus were produced a multitude of gaudy and fantastic appearances. But in the western or black chamber the effect of the fire-light that streamed upon the dark hangings through the blood-tinted panes, was ghastly in the extreme, and produced so wild a look upon the countenances of those who entered, that there were few of the company bold enough to set foot within its precincts at all.

It was in this apartment, also, that there stood against the western wall, a gigantic clock of ebony. Its pendulum swung to and fro with a dull, heavy, monotonous clang; and when the minute-hand made the circuit of the face, and the hour was to be stricken, there came from the brazen lungs of the clock a sound which was clear and loud and deep and exceedingly musical, but of so peculiar a note and emphasis that, at each lapse of an hour, the musicians of the orchestra were constrained to pause, momentarily, in their performance, to harken to the sound; and thus the waltzers perforce ceased their evolutions; and there was a brief disconcert of the whole gay company; and, while the chimes of the clock yet rang, it was observed that the giddiest grew pale, and the more aged and sedate passed their hands over their brows as if in confused reverie or meditation. But when the echoes had fully ceased, a light laughter at once pervaded the assembly; the musicians looked at each other and smiled as if at their own nervousness and folly, and made whispering vows, each to the other, that the next chiming of the clock should produce in them no similar emotion; and then, after the lapse of sixty minutes (which embrace three thousand and six hundred seconds of the Time that flies), there came yet another chiming of the clock, and then were the same disconcert and tremulousness and meditation as before.

COMMENTARY

The most westerly room, the seventh, is the exception. It has black velvet decorations but scarlet window panes. In it there is a huge grandfather clock. When it strikes the hour, its chime has a curious effect on the guests.

candelabrum: candle-holder with several branches
depended: hung
emanating: shining out
countenances: faces
precincts: walls
ebony: hard black wood

brazen: harsh-sounding, made of brass
constrained: forced against their will
perforce: of necessity
disconcert: feeling of upset
giddiest: liveliest, youngest
reverie: dreamy thoughts of the past
tremulousness: nervousness, unease

But, in spite of these things, it was a gay and magnificent revel. The tastes of the duke were peculiar. He had a fine eye for colours and effects. He disregarded the decora of mere fashion. His plans were bold and fiery, and his conceptions glowed with barbaric lustre. There are some who would have thought him mad. His followers felt that he was not. It was necessary to hear and see and touch him to be *sure* that he was not.

He had directed, in great part, the movable embellishments of the seven chambers, upon occasion of this great *fête*; and it was his own guiding taste which had given character to the masqueraders. Be sure they were grotesque. There were much glare and glitter and piquancy and phantasm – much of what has been since seen in 'Hernani'. There were arabesque figures with unsuited limbs and appointments. There were delirious fancies such as the madman fashions. There were much of the beautiful, much of the wanton, much of the *bizarre*, something of the terrible, and not a little of that which might have excited disgust. To and fro in the seven chambers there stalked, in fact, a multitude of dreams. And these – the dreams – writhed in and about, taking hue from the rooms, and causing the wild music of the orchestra to seem as the echo of their steps. And, anon, there strikes the ebony clock which stands in the hall of the velvet. And then, for a moment, all is still, and all is silent save the voice of the clock. The dreams are stiff-frozen as they stand. But the echoes of the chime die away – they have endured but an instant – and a light, half-subdued laughter floats after them as they depart. And now again, the music swells, and the dreams live, and writhe to and fro more merrily then ever, taking hue from the many tinted windows through which stream the rays from the tripods. But to the chamber which lies most westwardly of the seven, there are now none of the maskers who venture; for the night is waning away; and there flows a ruddier light through the blood-coloured panes: and the blackness of the sable drapery appals; and to him whose foot falls upon the sable carpet, there comes from the near clock of ebony a muffled peal more solemnly emphatic than any which reaches *their* ears who indulged in the more remote gaieties of the other apartments.

peculiar: distinctive
decora: trends, rules
embellishments: decorations
grotesque: weird, outrageous
piquancy: things that were both exciting and disturbing
phantasm: things that were like ghostly dreams
'Hernani': a tragedy by Victor Hugo
arabesque: fanciful, exotic
wanton: wild, riotous
anon: from time to time
sable: black material worn at funerals
gaieties: pleasures

COMMENTARY
The masked ball is spectacular. It reflects Prince Prospero's own love of pleasure: it is full of colour, wildness and fantasy. All the guests are urged to dress and behave in any way they wish – and they do.

But these other apartments were densely crowded, and in them beat feverishly the heart of life. And the revel went whirlingly on, until at length there commenced the sounding of midnight upon the clock. And then the music ceased, as I have told; and the evolutions of the waltzers were quieted; and there was an uneasy cessation of all things as before. But now there were twelve strokes to be sounded by the bell of the clock; and thus it happened, perhaps, that more of thought crept, with more of time, into the meditations of the thoughtful among those who revelled. And thus too, it happened, perhaps, that before the last echoes of the last chime had utterly sunk into silence, there were many individuals in the crowd who had found leisure to become aware of the presence of a masked figure which had arrested the attention of no single individual before. And the rumour of this new presence having spread itself whisperingly around, there arose at length from the whole company a buzz, or murmur, expressive of disapprobation and surprise – then, finally, of terror, of horror, and of disgust.

In an assembly of phantasms such as I have painted, it may well be supposed that no ordinary appearance could have excited such sensation. In truth the masquerade licence of the night was nearly unlimited; but the figure in question had out-Heroded Herod, and gone beyond the bounds of even the prince's indefinite decorum. There are chords in the hearts of the most reckless which cannot be touched without emotion. Even with the utterly lost, to whom life and death are equally jests, there are matters of which no jest can be made. The whole company, indeed, seemed now deeply to feel that in the costume and bearing of the stranger neither wit nor propriety existed. The figure was tall and gaunt, and shrouded from head to foot in the habiliments of the grave. The mask which concealed the visage was made so nearly to resemble the countenance of a stiffened corpse that the closest scrutiny must have had difficulty in detecting the cheat. And yet all this might have been endured, if not approved, by the mad revellers around. But the mummer had gone so far as to assume the type of the Red Death. His vesture was dabbled in *blood* – and his broad brow, with all the features of the face, was besprinkled with the scarlet horror.

COMMENTARY

When the ebony clock strikes midnight, the masque ends. Gradually, the guests become aware of a mysterious figure amongst them. He also wears a mask – but no one has noticed him before. He is dressed like the plague. The guests feel uneasy.

more of thought: a deeper seriousness
arrested: struck
disapprobation: dislike, disapproval
licence: what was allowed
out-Heroded Herod: made a stronger impression
indefinite decorum: easy-going morals
lost: sinful, damned

wit nor propriety: anything amusing or suitable for the occasion
habiliments of the grave: burial clothes for a dead body
scrutiny: inspection
assume the type of the Red Death: dress up as an image of the plague
vesture: costume

When the eyes of Prince Prospero fell upon this spectral image (which, with a slow and solemn movement, as if more fully to sustain its *rôle*, stalked to and fro among the waltzers) he was seen to be convulsed in the first moment with a strong shudder either of terror or distaste; but, in the next, his brow reddened with rage.

'Who dares,' he demanded hoarsely of the courtiers who stood near him – 'who dares insult us with this blasphemous mockery? Seize him and unmask him – that we may know whom we have to hang at sunrise, from the battlements!'

It was in the eastern or blue chamber in which stood the Prince Prospero as he uttered these words. They rang throughout the seven rooms loudly and clearly – for the prince was a bold and robust man, and the music had become hushed at the waving of his hand.

It was in the blue room where stood the prince, with a group of pale courtiers by his side. At first, as he spoke, there was a slight rushing movement of this group in the direction of the intruder, who at that moment was also near at hand, and now, with deliberate and stately step, made closer approach to the speaker. But from a certain nameless awe with which the mad assumptions of the mummer had inspired the whole party, there were found none who put forth hand to seize him; so that, unimpeded, he passed within a yard of the prince's person; and, while the vast assembly, as if with one impulse, shrank from the centres of the rooms to the walls, he made his way uninterruptedly, but with the same solemn and measured step which had distinguished him from the first, through the blue chamber to the purple – through the purple to the green – through the green to the orange – through this again to the white – and even thence to the violet, ere a decided movement had been made to arrest him. It was then, however, that the Prince Prospero, maddening with rage and the shame of his own momentary cowardice, rushed hurriedly through the six chambers, while none followed him on account of a deadly terror that had seized upon all. He bore aloft a drawn dagger, and had approached, in rapid impetuosity, to within three or

spectral image: ghostly vision
robust: fearless, strong-minded
nameless awe: indefinable dread
unimpeded: without being stopped
first: beginning
ere: before
impetuosity: violent rashness

COMMENTARY

Prince Prospero is furious. He orders the silent figure to be imprisoned and hung. However, no one dares to touch the stranger. The 'Red Death' moves like a ghost out of the room. Prince Prospero pursues him to the seventh room – the black one containing the ebony clock.

four feet of the retreating figure, when the latter, having attained the extremity of the velvet apartment, turned suddenly and confronted his pursuer. There was a sharp cry – and the dagger dropped gleaming upon the sable carpet, upon which, instantly afterwards, fell prostrate in death the Prince Prospero. Then, summoning the wild courage of despair, a throng of the revellers at once threw themselves into the black apartment, and, seizing the mummer, whose tall figure stood erect and motionless within the shadow of the ebony clock, gasped in unutterable horror at finding the grave cerements and corpse-like mask, which they handled with so violent a rudeness, untenanted by any tangible form.

And now was acknowledged the presence of the Red Death. He had come like a thief in the night. And one by one dropped the revellers in the blood-bedewed halls of their revel, and died each in the despairing posture of his fall. And the life of the ebony clock went out with that of the last of the gay. And the flames of the tripods expired. And Darkness and Decay and the Red Death held illimitable dominion over all.

PAUSE FOR PLAYBACK:
Now look at the playback questions on page 46.

COMMENTARY
The Prince raises his dagger, but when the ghostly figure looks him in the face he falls down dead. The guests grab the 'Red Death' figure to find that the clothes are empty – and, like their prince, they too die instantly.

summoning: calling up
cerements: burial clothes
untenanted by any tangible form: without a body inside
bedewed: soaked, splashed
illimitable dominion: unending power

Study guide

PAGES 39 TO 45:

➤ If you had been Prince Prospero, would you have reacted to the plague in the same way as he does? Why, or why not?

➤ Prince Prospero has had the fortified abbey built to his own design. What do its architecture and decoration suggest about his character?

➤ In how many ways is the seventh 'chamber' different from all the others?

➤ When the ebony clock strikes the hour, it has an unusual effect on all the guests. What is it?

* * * * *

➤ Re-read the description of the masked ball on page 42. If you had been one of the guests, do you think *you* would have enjoyed it?

➤ 'And the rumour of this new presence having spread itself whisperingly around' (page 43). Who is the 'new presence'? Where do you think he has come from?

➤ Why is it not possible to carry out Prince Prospero's orders to 'hang' the Stranger 'at sunrise'?

➤ Think about the title Poe has given to his story. Why do you think he chose it? Is it a good one?

REVIEWING THE WHOLE STORY: SUGGESTED ACTIVITIES

1 'Time that flies'

In *The Masque of the Red Death*, there are many references to time and its passing. This activity asks you to explore the theme of time in the story as a whole.

a **By yourself**, find whereabouts in the text these three quotations come from:

- 'And the whole seizure, progress, and termination of the disease, were the incidents of half an hour.'

- 'Its pendulum swung to and fro with a dull, heavy monotonous clang; and when the minute-hand made the circuit of the face, and the hour was to be stricken, there came from the brazen lungs of the clock a sound which was clear and loud and deep'.

- 'And the life of the ebony clock went out with that of the last of the gay.'

Apart from the obvious point, what do these quotations have in common?

b **As a class**, build up from this starting-point a list of *every* reference to time, and every comment about it, that the author makes. You may be surprised by how many you find. Keep a record of them in note form.

c **In a group**, use your class list to talk about *why* Poe seems so concerned with time in his story. Here are two suggestions – you are likely to think of others:

- He wants us to see that human life is at the mercy of time and can be stopped very suddenly, in the way a clock sometimes stops.

- There is no escape for us from the destructive effect of time, however much we may throw ourselves into trying to avoid it.

d **In a class discussion**, plan a written account of what Poe is saying about 'Time that flies' in *The Masque of the Red Death*. The exact title is best decided with your teacher, depending on how your discussion goes. No matter how you write your account, however, make sure you link your comments closely to the events described in the story.

Draw on the text-study you have done throughout this activity to find quotations for your writing. Use them to illustrate the main points you make.

2 | Statements: true, false, or...?

Below are five statements about *The Masque of the Red Death*. Use your own response to the story to decide how far you agree with them. There are no 'right' or 'wrong' answers. The purpose of this activity is for you to put forward your *own* ideas and to argue your case.

a **By yourself**, consider each of the statements in turn. Make notes to show why you 'agree', 'disagree' or 'partly agree'.

> **Statement 1**
> Although he is described as bold and fearless, Prince Prospero is actually a miserable coward.

> **Statement 2**
> The story shows how the upper classes carry on enjoying themselves and wasting money whilst the poor people are left to struggle on their own.

> **Statement 3**
> The reason why the figure of the Red Death is dressed in grave-clothes is to show the guests that the plague will sooner or later wipe out everyone in the kingdom.

> **Statement 4**
> The ending of the story is a big let-down. It just isn't realistic to have 1,000 people dying because someone dressed as the Red Death plays a clever conjuring trick.

> **Statement 5**
> There is only one occasion when a character speaks; otherwise the story is all description. It would be more interesting to read if there were a better balance between the two.

b Hold a **class (or group) discussion** in which you use your notes to say what you think about the statements. Listen to other people's views, including those that differ from yours. When you give your own opinions, explain them as fully as you can, referring back to parts of the text. Don't be content to say just a few words!

3 | Building up the atmosphere

Few readers of *The Masque of the Red Death* ever forget the *atmosphere* of the story. This activity asks you (i) to describe what its atmosphere is like and (ii) to examine the ways in which Poe builds it up.

a   **With a partner**, scan the whole story looking for evidence that, at certain points, the atmosphere is:

- mysterious
- violent
- frightening
- supernatural
- tense
- grotesque.

Find at least two quotations – they need not be long ones – to illustrate each of the above. Keep a careful note of them.

b   **In a group**, compare your findings. Then try to agree, with reasons, on a 'rank order' for the six descriptions of the story's atmosphere listed in **a**. So: if you think that the atmosphere is more 'mysterious' than anything else, put that as Number 1. On the other hand, if you think that 'grotesque' describes the story's atmosphere less well than any of the other words, put that as Number 6. You may decide that some of the words listed are of equal importance.

c   **As a class**, look in careful detail at these two extracts:

- The whole paragraph beginning 'It was a voluptuous scene, that masquerade' (pages 40 to 41).
- The whole paragraph beginning 'It was in the blue room where stood the prince' (pages 44 to 45).

Discuss how many of the 'atmosphere words' in **a** apply to the description in these paragraphs. Be very precise: focus on small details, single words and phrases, and on Poe's choices of language to picture the scene.

Are there any more 'atmosphere words' you now wish to add to the list? If there are, do so.

d   **By yourself**, choose *three* atmosphere words which you think apply best to *The Masque of the Red Death*. For each, write a paragraph demonstrating how Poe creates the atmosphere they describe. To do this well, you *must* examine – and quote from – the text as fully as possible.

THE CASK OF AMONTILLADO

Look out for...
- **the narrator's reasons for taking revenge on Fortunato.**
- **how the narrator lures Fortunato to his doom.**
- **the way in which the story's setting helps create a mood of horror.**

The thousand injuries of Fortunato I had borne as best I could; but when he ventured upon insult I vowed revenge. You, who so well know the nature of my soul, will not suppose, however, that I gave utterance to a threat. *At length* I would be avenged; this was a point definitely settled – but the very definitiveness with which it was resolved precluded the idea of risk. I must not only punish but punish with impunity. A wrong is unredressed when retribution overtakes its redresser. It is equally unredressed when the avenger fails to make himself felt as such to him who has done the wrong.

It must be understood that neither by word nor deed had I given Fortunato cause to doubt my good will. I continued, as was my wont, to smile in his face, and he did not perceive that my smile *now* was at the thought of his immolation.

He had a weak point – this Fortunato – although in other regards he was a man to be respected and even feared. He prided himself on his connoisseurship in wine. Few Italians have the true virtuoso spirit. For the most part their enthusiasm is adopted to suit the time and opportunity – to practise imposture upon the British and American *millionaires*. In painting and gemmary, Fortunato, like his countrymen, was a quack – but in the matter of

COMMENTARY

The narrator has a grievance against Fortunato. He vows to punish him for it. Fortunato has a weakness that the narrator will exploit: he prides himself on being an expert on fine wines.

Amontillado: a superior kind of white wine
precluded: counted out
with impunity: without fear of the consequences
unredressed when retribution overtakes its redresser: not put right if the avenger is punished
wont: custom, habit
immolation: death
connoisseurship: expertise
virtuoso spirit: flair in their character
imposture: deceit
gemmary: precious stones
quack: fraud

old wines he was sincere. In this respect I did not differ from him materially; I was skilful in the Italian vintages myself, and bought largely whenever I could.

It was about dusk, one evening during the supreme madness of the carnival season, that I encountered my friend. He accosted me with excessive warmth, for he had been drinking much. The man wore motley. He had on a tight-fitting parti-striped dress, and his head was surmounted by the conical cap and bells. I was so pleased to see him that I thought I should never have done wringing his hand.

I said to him – 'My dear Fortunato, you are luckily met. How remarkably well you are looking to-day. But I have received a pipe of what passes for Amontillado, and I have my doubts.'

'How?' said he. 'Amontillado? A pipe? Impossible! And in the middle of the carnival!'

'I have my doubts,' I replied; 'and I was silly enough to pay the full Amontillado price without consulting you in the matter. You were not to be found, and I was fearful of losing a bargain.'

'Amontillado!'

'I have my doubts.'

'Amontillado!'

'And I must satisfy them.'

'Amontillado!'

'As you are engaged, I am on my way to Luchesi. If any one has a critical turn it is he. He will tell me –'

'Luchesi cannot tell Amontillado from Sherry.'

'And yet some fool will have it that his taste is a match for your own.'

'Come, let us go.'

'Whither?'

'To your vaults.'

'My friend, no; I will not impose upon your good nature. I perceive you have an engagement. Luchesi –'

'I have no engagement; – come.'

accosted: greeted
motley: a jester's costume
dress: outfit
pipe: case, box
Luchesi: another wine expert
critical turn: reliable taste, good judgement
vaults: wine cellars

COMMENTARY

There is a carnival in the town. Fortunato, dressed up as a jester, has been drinking heavily when the narrator meets him. He is readily persuaded to give his opinion on whether some Amontillado the narrator has just bought is the genuine article.

'My friend, no. It is not the engagement, but the severe cold with which I perceive you are afflicted. The vaults are insufferably damp. They are encrusted with nitre.'

'Let us go, nevertheless. The cold is merely nothing. Amontillado! You have been imposed upon. And as for Luchesi, he cannot distinguish Sherry from Amontillado.'

Thus speaking, Fortunato possessed himself of my arm; and putting on a mask of black silk and drawing a *roquelaire* closely about my person, I suffered him to hurry me to my palazzo.

There were no attendants at home; they had absconded to make merry in honour of the time. I had told them that I should not return until the morning, and had given them explicit orders not to stir from the house. These orders were sufficient, I well knew, to insure their immediate disappearance, one and all, as soon as my back was turned.

I took from their sconces two flambeaux, and giving one to Fortunato, bowed him through several suites of rooms to the archway that led to the vaults. I passed down a long and winding staircase, requesting him to be cautious as he followed. We came at length to the foot of the descent, and stood together on the damp ground of the catacombs of the Montresors.

The gait of my friend was unsteady, and the bells upon his cap jingled as he strode.

'The pipe,' said he.

'It is farther on,' said I; 'but observe the white web-work which gleams from these cavern walls.'

He turned towards me, and looked into my eyes with two filmy orbs that distilled the rheum of intoxication.

'Nitre?' he asked at length.

'Nitre,' I replied. 'How long have you had that cough?'

'Ugh! ugh! ugh! – ugh! ugh! ugh! – ugh! ugh! ugh! – ugh! ugh! ugh! – ugh! ugh! ugh!'

My poor friend found it impossible to reply for many minutes.

COMMENTARY

To find the newly bought Amontillado, the narrator and Fortunato go down to the narrator's cellars. These also house the remains of his ancestors. Fortunato is feverish as well as drunk.

afflicted: suffering

nitre: saltpetre (which gives an unhealthy coating to the walls)

imposed upon: sold short, taken in

roquelaire: long cloak

palazzo: mansion

absconded: sneaked away to the carnival

sconces: torch-holders

flambeaux: flaming torches

catacombs of the Montresors: tombs of the narrator's family

gait: manner of walking

distilled the rheum of intoxication: gleamed dully with drunkenness

'It is nothing,' he said, at last.

'Come,' I said with decision, 'we will go back; your health is precious. You are rich, respected, admired, beloved; you are happy, as once I was. You are a man to be missed. For me it is no matter. We will go back; you will be ill, and I cannot be responsible. Besides, there is Luchesi! –'

'Enough,' he said; 'the cough is a mere nothing; it will not kill me. I shall not die of a cough.'

'True – true,' I replied; 'and, indeed, I had no intention of alarming you unnecessarily – but you should use all proper caution. A draught of this Medoc will defend us from the damps.'

Here I knocked off the neck of a bottle which I drew from a long row of its fellows that lay upon the mould.

'Drink,' I said, presenting him the wine.

He raised it to his lips with a leer. He paused and nodded to me familiarly, while his bells jingled.

'I drink,' he said, 'to the buried that repose around us.'

'And I to your long life.'

He again took my arm, and we proceeded.

'These vaults,' he said, 'are extensive.'

'The Montresors,' I replied, 'were a great and numerous family.'

'I forget your arms.'

'A huge human foot d'or, in a field azure; the foot crushes a serpent rampant whose fangs are embedded in the heel.'

'And the motto?'

'*Nemo me impune lacessit.*'

'Good!' he said.

The wine sparkled in his eyes and the bells jingled. My own fancy grew warm with the Medoc. We had passed through walls of piled bones, with casks and puncheons intermingling, into the inmost recesses of the catacombs. I paused again, and this time I made bold to seize Fortunato by an arm above the elbow.

A draught of this Medoc: A drink of this
   French red wine
leer: smiling grimace
repose: rest in peace
arms: i.e. coat of arms
d'or: of gold
'Nemo me impune lacessit': No one
   provokes me without being punished
fancy: imagination
puncheons: huge barrels

COMMENTARY
The narrator pretends to be worried about Fortunato's health and suggests they go back. He knows this will only increase the determination of his 'friend' to proceed further into the vaults. It does.

'The nitre!' I said; 'see, it increases. It hangs like moss upon the vaults. We are below the river's bed. The drops of moisture trickle among the bones. Come, we will go back ere it is too late. Your cough –'

'It is nothing,' he said; 'let us go on. But first, another draught of the Medoc.'

I broke and reached him a flagon of De Grâve. He emptied it at a breath. His eyes flashed with a fierce light. He laughed and threw the bottle upwards with a gesticulation I did not understand.

I looked at him in surprise. He repeated the movement – a grotesque one.

'You do not comprehend?' he said.

'Not I,' I replied.

'Then you are not of the brotherhood?'

'How?'

'You are not of the masons?'

'Yes, yes,' I said; 'yes, yes.'

'You? Impossible! A mason?'

'A mason,' I replied.

'A sign,' he said, 'a sign.'

'It is this,' I answered, producing a trowel from beneath the folds of my *roquelaire*.

'You jest,' he exclaimed, recoiling a few paces. 'But let us proceed to the Amontillado.'

'Be it so,' I said, replacing the tool beneath the cloak, and again offering him my arm. He leaned upon it heavily. We continued our route in search of the Amontillado. We passed through a range of low arches, descended, passed on, and descending again, arrived at a deep crypt, in which the foulness of the air caused our flambeaux rather to glow than flame.

At the most remote end of the crypt there appeared another less spacious.

Its walls had been lined with human remains, piled to the vault overhead, in the fashion of the great catacombs of Paris. Three sides of this interior crypt were still ornamented in this manner. From the fourth the bones had been

COMMENTARY

The two men go deeper and deeper into the cellars. The air grows damper and more unwholesome. Fortunato is astonished when the narrator produces a trowel to show that, like him, he is a Freemason. Finally they reach a deep burial vault.

ere: before

flagon: bottle

gesticulation: hand movement

grotesque: weird, very strange

brotherhood: a secret society known as the Freemasons

trowel: one of the symbols of Freemasonry

recoiling: stepping back

crypt: burial chamber

thrown down, and lay promiscuously upon the earth, forming at one point a mound of some size. Within the wall thus exposed by the displacing of the bones, we perceived a still interior recess, in depth about four feet, in width three, in height six or seven. It seemed to have been constructed for no especial use within itself, but formed merely the interval between two of the colossal supports of the roof of the catacombs, and was backed by one of their circumscribing walls of solid granite.

It was in vain that Fortunato, uplifting his dull torch, endeavoured to pry into the depth of the recess. Its termination the feeble light did not enable us to see.

'Proceed,' I said; 'herein is the Amontillado. As for Luchesi –'

'He is an ignoramus,' interrupted my friend, as he stepped unsteadily forward, while I followed immediately at his heels. In an instant he had reached the extremity of the niche, and finding his progress arrested by the rock, stood stupidly bewildered. A moment more and I had fettered him to the granite. In its surface were two iron staples, distant from each other by about two feet, horizontally. From one of these depended a short chain, from the other a padlock. Throwing the links about his waist, it was but the work of a few seconds to secure it. He was too much astounded to resist. Withdrawing the key I stepped back from the recess.

'Pass your hand,' I said, 'over the wall; you cannot help feeling the nitre. Indeed, it is very damp. Once more let me *implore* you to return. No? Then I must positively leave you. But I must first render you all the little attentions in my power.'

'The Amontillado!' ejaculated my friend, not yet recovered from his astonishment.

'True,' I replied; 'the Amontillado.'

As I said these words I busied myself among the pile of bones of which I have spoken before. Throwing them aside, I soon uncovered a quantity of building stone and mortar. With these materials and with the aid of my trowel, I began vigorously to wall up the entrance to the niche.

promiscuously: loosely scattered
still interior: even deeper
circumscribing: surrounding
termination: far end
arrested: blocked
fettered: bound, chained up
depended: hung
positively: most certainly
ejaculated: exclaimed

COMMENTARY
The vault is lined with human remains. At its far end is a recess in which the narrator claims the Amontillado is stored. Fortunato steps in – and the narrator quickly shackles him, by a chain and padlock, to the wall.

I had scarcely laid the first tier of the masonry when I discovered that the intoxication of Fortunato had in a great measure worn off. The earliest indication I had of this was a low moaning cry from the depth of the recess.

It was *not* the cry of a drunken man. There was then a long and obstinate silence. I laid the second tier, and the third, and the fourth; and then I heard the furious vibrations of the chain. The noise lasted for several minutes, during which, that I might hearken to it with the more satisfaction, I ceased my labours and sat down upon the bones. When at last the clanking subsided, I resumed the trowel, and finished without interruption the fifth, sixth and the seventh tier. The wall was now nearly upon a level with my breast. I again paused, and holding the flambeaux over the mason-work, threw a few feeble rays upon the figure within.

A succession of loud and shrill screams, bursting suddenly from the throat of the chained form, seemed to thrust me violently back. For a brief moment I hesitated – I trembled. Unsheathing my rapier, I began to grope with it about the recess; but the thought of an instant reassured me. I placed my hand upon the solid fabric of the catacombs, and felt satisfied. I reapproached the wall. I replied to the yells of him who clamoured. I re-echoed – I aided – I surpassed them in volume and in strength. I did this, and the clamourer grew still.

It was now midnight, and my task was drawing to a close. I had completed the eighth, the ninth, and the tenth tier. I had finished a portion of the last and the eleventh; there remained but a single stone to be fitted and plastered in. I struggled with its weight; I placed it partially in its destined position. But now there came from out the niche a low laugh that erected the hairs upon my head. It was succeeded by a sad voice, which I had difficulty in recognising as that of the noble Fortunato. The voice said –

'Ha! ha! ha! – he! he! – a very good joke, indeed – an excellent jest. We will have many a rich laugh about it at the palazzo – he! he! he! – over our wine – he! he! he!'

'The Amontillado!' I said.

'He! he! he! – he! he! he! – yes, the Amontillado. But is it not getting late?

COMMENTARY

The narrator begins to wall Fortunato into the recess at the far end of the vault. Fortunato rattles his chains and screams but finally, his screams stop. Just before the final stone is put in place, Fortunato speaks. He congratulates the narrator on playing a practical joke on him, and looks forward to laughing about it over a bottle of...Amontillado.

tier: layer of stones
hearken: listen
rapier: long sharp-pointed sword
destined: intended

Will not they be awaiting us at the palazzo, the Lady Fortunato and the rest?
Let us be gone.'

'Yes,' I said, 'let us be gone.'

'*For the love of God, Montresor!*'

'Yes,' I said, 'for the love of God!'

But to these words I hearkened in vain for a reply. I grew impatient. I called
aloud –

'Fortunato!'

No answer. I called again –

'Fortunato!'

No answer still. I thrust a torch through the remaining aperture and let it
fall within. There came forth in return only a jingling of the bells. My heart
grew sick – on account of the dampness of the catacombs. I hastened to make
an end of my labour. I forced the last stone into its position; I plastered it up.
Against the new masonry I re-erected the old rampart of bones. For half of a
century no mortal has disturbed them. *In pace requiescat!*

PAUSE FOR PLAYBACK:
Now look at the playback questions on page 59.

---

aperture: hole in the brickwork
rampart: barricade
In pace requiescat!: Rest in peace!

COMMENTARY
The narrator forces the final stone into
place – Fortunato will not drink again.

Study guide

PAGES 51 TO 58:

➤ At the start of the story, the narrator says that Fortunato has done him a great many wrongs. Why, then, does he continue to 'smile in his face' (page 51)?

➤ What is Fortunato wearing when the narrator meets him? He continues to wear the same clothes throughout the rest of the story. Why do you think Poe chooses to present him in this way?

➤ Why does the narrator keep mentioning Luchesi, an expert on fine wines?

➤ When they are in the cellars, the narrator keeps encouraging Fortunato to drink (e.g. 'A draught of this Medoc will protect us from the damps' – page 54). Why?

* * * * *

➤ Remind yourself of what the narrator's coat of arms is like (page 54). What does his family motto mean? Can you apply either or both of these to anything that happens in the story?

➤ How, exactly, does the narrator manage to get Fortunato into the recess and bind him up?

➤ 'Once more let me *implore* you to return' (page 56). How is Fortunato likely to react to this comment by the narrator? What does it show about the narrator's character?

➤ What feelings does the narrator have while he is walling up Fortunato in the recess? What feelings doesn't he have that you might expect him to?

REVIEWING THE WHOLE STORY: SUGGESTED ACTIVITIES

1 Putting on a mask

As he leads Fortunato to his home, the narrator says: 'Putting on a mask of black silk..., I suffered him to hurry' (page 53). The narrator also wears a second mask: the mask of deceit and untruth.

This activity asks you to trace and explain all the deceptions by which the narrator leads Fortunato to his death.

a   **By yourself**, skim the story from 'It was about dusk' (page 52) to the end. Make a mental note of the ways in which Fortunato is deceived, or 'taken in', by the narrator.

b   **With a partner**, use a large sheet of paper to make a 'lie chart', like this:

Narrator's lie/deception	Explanation for it
1. Pretends to be glad to see F at the carnival, although he hates him	So that...
2 Tells F he has just bought a case of Amontillado	So that...

You should be able to list ten or more examples.

c   **As a class**, talk about your findings. As well as comparing lists, put forward your views on:

  • why Fortunato is so often, and so easily, taken in, *and*

  • what this shows about his character.

d   **By yourself**, write an account of 'How Fortunato is lured to his death'. Wherever possible, quote from the text to back up the points you make.

2 The ghost of Fortunato: a radio drama

During the story, the narrator shows no sign of a guilty conscience. Imagine that after Fortunato dies he haunts the narrator – in order to make him realise the horror of what he has done.

a   **In a group**, plan and perform a ten-minute radio drama entitled 'The Ghost of Fortunato'.

When planning it, think about and discuss:

- the way in which Fortunato would describe exactly how he died.

- the places in which, and the times when, he would choose to haunt his murderer.

- what he would accuse the narrator of.

- how he would try to make his murderer feel guilty.

- how the narrator would react to being haunted (it can be on more than one occasion).

- how your drama should end.

b   Decide how to make the drama as effective as possible by considering:

- how to make clear to listeners who don't know the story what is happening.

- how you are going to use different voices and sound-effects (including music, if you wish).

- how to divide up the performance between you.

- and anything else you think is important.

c   When you feel well prepared, talk with your teacher about what you have planned. Listen carefully to his/her comments and consider making any changes in the light of these.

d   Perform your drama onto audio tape. You are responsible for organising everything and for making sure it sounds as professional as possible. If it goes wrong, stop and begin again – but you are limited to *three* attempts at the most!

e   When you have finished, **join up with another group**. Listen to each other's tapes. Say honestly how successful you think they have turned out to be, giving constructive reasons for what you decide.

Your teacher may wish to use this activity to assess your Speaking and Listening skills.

3 | 'I vowed revenge'

The Cask of Amontillado is a 'revenge story'. At the start, the narrator says that Fortunato has given him 'a thousand injuries' for which he has sworn to pay him back.

You will have noticed, however, that the narrator never tells us directly what these 'injuries' or 'wrongs' are. The reader has to work them out, or to imagine them, by picking up hints from the story.

a **By yourself**, skim the story looking for any reasons as to why the narrator feels such a strong grudge against Fortunato – a grudge *so* strong that he kills him for it.

b **As a class**, discuss your findings. In your opinion, are the 'hints' you have found sufficient to explain and justify what the narrator does to Fortunato?

c **In a group**, imagine what *may* have happened before the start of the story to account for the narrator's hatred of Fortunato. Base what you say on reading 'between the lines' of Poe's story. As you talk, you should each make a 'note circle' like the one below. Your circles need not be the same. Use as many segments as you wish.

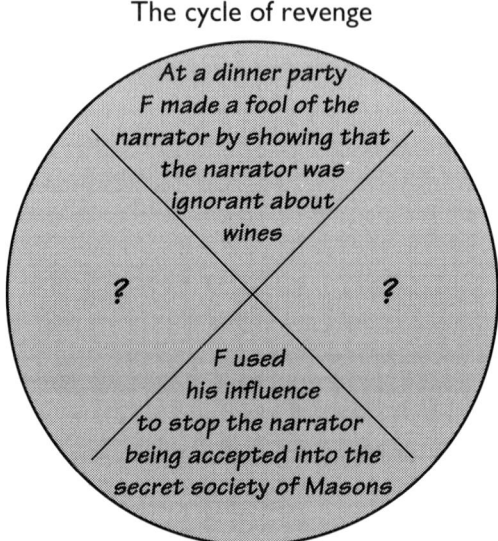

The cycle of revenge

At a dinner party F made a fool of the narrator by showing that the narrator was ignorant about wines

?   ?

F used his influence to stop the narrator being accepted into the secret society of Masons

d **By yourself**, write an account of the past relationship between Fortunato and the narrator to explain why the former is murdered by the latter. Invent your own title. Use a writing style which you think is best suited to what you are describing.

1 A sense of place

Almost everything that happens in *The Cask of Amontillado* takes place in the cellars beneath the narrator's house. In this activity, you are asked to explore why Poe chooses this **setting** for the story, and to decide what use he makes of it.

a **With a partner**, draw a 'story route-map' to show the journey taken by the narrator and Fortunato. Start with their chance meeting at the carnival. End in the recess where Fortunato is walled up.

Label your route-map carefully. In particular, look closely at the different stages of their journey through the house and the cellars. There are at least five separate parts of the cellar-system which need to be marked on your map.

When labelling, note briefly (i) what happens at each 'stopping point' (or 'location') and (ii) what the surroundings are like. It doesn't matter if you can't draw brilliantly: stick-insect figures and symbols are quite sufficient. It will help if you use colour to suggest the atmosphere of every place you mark.

b Refer to your route-map to take part in a **class discussion** about Poe's use of settings in the story. Amongst other things, talk about:

- how, as the journey goes on, each setting in sequence becomes more gloomy, sinister and horrific.
- how each setting in sequence reveals more and more about the narrator's feelings towards Fortunato.

c **In a group**, imagine you have been asked to direct a film of *The Cask of Amontillado*.

Choose three different settings from anywhere in the story. Discuss how you would film them. As you talk, you should each jot down notes about the following things, which are the director's responsibility:

- the scenery and how you would use it in the film.
- the lighting for each of the three settings you've chosen.
- any sound-effects you require.
- camera shots (e.g. tracking-shots, panning-shots, close-ups).

d **By yourself**, turn the notes you have made in group discussion into a 'director's shooting script'. Write about how you would film your three chosen settings in a way that is true to Poe's story.

If you are particularly interested in films and filming, you could extend this piece of writing into a shooting script for a film of the whole story. Discuss it with your teacher.

'THOU ART THE MAN'

Look out for…
- **the circumstances surrounding Mr Shuttleworthy's murder.**
- **the part played by Charley Goodfellow in searching for the dead body.**
- **the character and reputation of Pennifeather, the murdered man's nephew.**

I will now play the Oedipus to the Rattleborough enigma. I will expound – as I alone can – the secret of the enginery that effected the Rattleborough miracle – the one, the true, the admitted, the undisputed, the indisputable miracle, which put a definite end to infidelity among the Rattleburghers, and converted to the orthodoxy of the grandames all the carnal-minded who had ventured to be sceptical before.

This event – which I should be sorry to discuss in a tone of unsuitable levity – occurred in the summer of 18——. Mr Barnabas Shuttleworthy – one of the wealthiest and most respectable citizens of the borough – had been missing for several days under circumstances which gave rise to suspicion of foul play. Mr Shuttleworthy had set out from Rattleborough very early one Saturday morning, on horseback, with the avowed intention of proceeding to the city of ——, about fifteen miles distant, and of returning the night of the same day. Two hours after his departure, however, his horse returned without him, and without the saddle-bags which had been strapped on his back at starting. The animal was wounded, too, and covered with mud. These

COMMENTARY
A well-known resident of Rattleborough, Mr Shuttleworthy, has not returned from visiting a nearby town. His horse has come back without him. Foul play is suspected.

Oedipus: a famous solver of riddles
the Rattleborough enigma: the town's great mystery
enginery that effected: factors which lay behind
converted to...carnal-minded: made all the sinners behave well again
sceptical: morally slack
levity: humour, light-heartedness
avowed: stated, promised

circumstances naturally gave rise to much alarm among the friends of the missing man; and when it was found, on Sunday morning, that he had not yet made his appearance, the whole borough arose *en masse* to go and look for his body.

The foremost and most energetic in instituting this search was the bosom friend of Mr Shuttleworthy – a Mr Charles Goodfellow, or, as he was universally called, 'Charley Goodfellow', or 'Old Charley Goodfellow.' Now, whether it is a marvellous coincidence, or whether it is that the name itself has an imperceptible effect upon the character, I have never yet been able to ascertain; but the fact is unquestionable, that there never yet was any person named Charles who was not an open, manly, honest, good-natured, and frank-hearted fellow, with a rich, clear voice, that did you good to hear it, and an eye that looked you always straight in the face, as much as to say: 'I have a clear conscience myself, am afraid of no man, and am altogether above doing a mean action.' And thus all the hearty, careless, 'walking gentlemen' of the stage are very certain to be called Charles.

Now, 'Old Charley Goodfellow', although he had been in Rattleborough not longer than six months or thereabouts, and although nobody knew any thing about him before he came to settle in the neighbourhood, had experienced no difficulty in the world in making the acquaintance of all the respectable people in the borough. Not a man of them but would have taken his bare word for a thousand at any moment; and as for the women, there is no saying what they would not have done to oblige him. And all this came of him having been christened Charles, and of his possessing, in consequence, that ingenuous face which is proverbially the very 'best letter of recommendation.'

I have already said that Mr Shuttleworthy was one of the most respectable, and, undoubtedly, he was the most wealthy man in Rattleborough, while 'Old Charley Goodfellow' was upon as intimate terms with him as if he had been his own brother. The two old gentlemen were next-door neighbours, and, although Mr Shuttleworthy seldom, if ever, visited 'Old Charley,' and never

instituting: setting up
universally: i.e. by everyone
imperceptible: secret, subtle
taken his bare word for a thousand: bet
    $1,000 on him being trustworthy
oblige: please
ingenuous: honest
proverbially: always said to be
intimate: close and friendly

COMMENTARY
A search is suggested. After all, Mr Shuttleworthy is the richest man in Rattleborough. His close friend and neighbour is Charley Goodfellow. He has moved to the town only recently – but he is already liked and respected by everyone.

was known to take a meal in his house, still this did not prevent the two friends from being exceedingly intimate, as I have just observed; for 'Old Charley' never let a day pass without stepping in three or four times to see how his neighbour came on, and very often he would stay to breakfast or tea, and almost always to dinner; and then the amount of wine that was made way with by the two cronies at a sitting it would really be a difficult thing to ascertain. 'Old Charley's' favourite beverage was Château Margaux, and it appeared to do Mr Shuttleworthy's heart good to see the old fellow swallow it, as he did, quart after quart; so that, one day, when the wine was in and the wit, as a natural consequence, somewhat *out*, he said to his crony, as he slapped him on the back: 'I tell you what it is, Old Charley, you are, by all odds, the heartiest old fellow I ever came across in all my born days; and since you love to guzzle the wine at that fashion, I'll be darned if I don't have to make thee a present of a big box of the Château Margaux, Od rot me,' – (Mr Shuttleworthy had a sad habit of swearing, although he seldom went beyond 'Od rot me,' or 'By gosh,' or 'By the jolly golly,') – 'Od rot me,' says he, 'if I don't send an order to town this very afternoon for a double box of the best that can be got, and I'll make ye a present of it. I will! – ye needn't say a word now – I *will*, I tell ye, and there's an end of it; so look out for it – it will come to hand some of these fine days, precisely when ye are looking for it the least!' I mention this little bit of liberality on the part of Mr Shuttleworthy, just by way of showing you how *very* intimate an understanding existed between the two friends.

Well, on the Sunday morning in question, when it came to be fairly understood that Mr Shuttleworthy had met with foul play, I never saw any one so profoundly affected as 'Old Charley Goodfellow'. When he first heard that the horse had come home without his master, and without his master's saddle-bags, and all bloody from a pistol shot, that had gone clean through and through the poor animal's chest without quite killing him, – when he heard all this, he turned as pale as if the missing man had been his own dear brother or father, and shivered and shook all over as if he had had a fit of the ague.

COMMENTARY
When Mr Shuttleworthy's horse is found to be half-dead with a bullet wound, Charley is terribly upset. Apart from being his best friend, Mr Shuttleworthy is his drinking companion and has recently offered to buy him a double box of his favourite wine.

came on: was getting on
made way with: consumed
somewhat out: when Mr Shuttleworthy was rather tipsy
by all odds: by any standards
Od rot me: God damn me
liberality: generosity
fit of the ague: bout of fever

At first he was too much overpowered with grief to be able to do any thing at all, or to decide upon any plan of action; so that for a long time he endeavoured to dissuade Mr Shuttleworthy's other friends from making a stir about the matter, thinking it best to wait awhile – say for a week or two, or a month or two – to see if something wouldn't turn up, or if Mr Shuttleworthy wouldn't come in the natural way, and explain his reasons for sending his horse on before. I dare say you have often observed this disposition to temporise, or to procrastinate, in people who are labouring under any very poignant sorrow. Their powers of mind seem to be rendered torpid, so that they have a horror of any thing like action, and like nothing in the world so well as to lie quietly in bed and 'nurse their grief', as the old ladies express it – that is to say, ruminate over their trouble.

The people of Rattleborough had, indeed, so high an opinion of the wisdom and discretion of 'Old Charley,' that the greater part of them felt disposed to agree with him, and not make a stir in the business 'until something should turn up,' as the honest gentleman worded it; and I believe that, after all, this would have been the general determination, but for the very suspicious interference of Mr Shuttleworthy's nephew, a young man of very dissipated habits, and otherwise of rather bad character. This nephew, whose name was Pennifeather, would listen to nothing like reason in the matter of 'lying quiet', but insisted upon making immediate search for the 'corpse of the murdered man'. This was the expression, he employed; and Mr Goodfellow acutely remarked at the time, that it was 'a *singular* expression, to say no more.' This remark of 'Old Charley's', too, had great effect on the crowd; and one of the party was heard to ask, very impressively, 'how it happened that young Mr Pennifeather was so intimately cognisant of all the circumstances connected with his uncle's disappearance, as to feel authorised to assert, distinctly and unequivocally, that his uncle *was* a "murdered man".' Hereupon some little squibbling and bickering occurred among various members of the crowd, and especially between 'Old Charley' and Mr Pennifeather – although this latter occurrence was, indeed, by no means a novelty, for little good-will had

disposition to temporise, or to procrastinate:
   tendency to put things off
poignant: painful
rendered torpid: made sluggish
ruminate: ponder, think deeply
not make a stir: do nothing
determination: decision
dissipated: immoral
acutely: shrewdly, intelligently
singular: striking, unusual
cognisant of: knowledgeable about
unequivocally: without doubt
squibbling: disagreement

COMMENTARY
At first, Charley advises that everyone should wait to see if Mr Shuttleworthy, or some news about him, comes to light. However, Mr Pennifeather, Shuttleworthy's nephew, insists on an immediate search.

subsisted between the parties for the last three or four months; and matters had even gone so far that Mr Pennifeather had actually knocked down his uncle's friend for some alleged excess of liberty that the latter had taken in the uncle's house, of which the nephew was an inmate. Upon this occasion 'Old Charley' is said to have behaved with exemplary moderation and Christian charity. He arose from the blow, adjusted his clothes, and made no attempt at retaliation at all – merely muttering a few words about 'taking summary vengeance at the first convenient opportunity,' – a natural and very justifiable ebullition of anger, which meant nothing, however, and, beyond doubt, was no sooner given vent to than forgotten.

However these matters may be (which have no reference to the point now at issue), it is quite certain that the people of Rattleborough, principally through the persuasion of Mr Pennifeather, came at length to the determination of dispersing over the adjacent country in search of the missing Mr Shuttleworthy. I say they came to this determination in the first instance. After it had been fully resolved that a search should be made, it was considered almost a matter of course that the seekers should disperse – that is to say, distribute themselves in parties – for the more thorough examination of the region round about. I forget, however, by what ingenious train of reasoning it was that 'Old Charley' finally convinced the assembly that this was the most injudicious plan that could be pursued. Convince them, however, he did – all except Mr Pennifeather, and, in the end, it was arranged that a search should be instituted, carefully and very thoroughly, by the burghers en masse, 'Old Charley' himself leading the way.

As for the matter of that, there could have been no better pioneer than 'Old Charley', whom everybody knew to have the eye of a lynx; but, although he led them into all manner of out-of-the-way holes and corners, by routes that nobody had ever suspected of existing in the neighbourhood, and although the search was incessantly kept up day and night for nearly a week still no trace of Mr Shuttleworthy could be discovered. When I say no trace, however, I must not be understood to speak literally; for trace, to some extent, there certainly

---

COMMENTARY

A search finally begins. Pennifeather objects to Charley leading it. There is no love lost between these two. Not long before, he and Charley had a fight in Mr Shuttleworthy's house. Charley lost – and vowed revenge.

of which the nephew was an inmate: where Pennifeather lived
exemplary moderation: perfect restraint
summary: swift, decisive
ebullition: overflow
dispersing: spreading out
ingenious train of reasoning: subtle line of argument
injudicious: unwise
burghers: townspeople
incessantly: continuously

was. The poor gentleman had been tracked, by his horse's shoes (which were peculiar), to a spot about three miles to the east of the borough, on the main road leading to the city. Here the track made off into a by-path through a piece of woodland – the path coming out again into the main road, and cutting off about half a mile of the regular distance. Following the shoe-marks down this lane, the party came at length to a pool of stagnant water, half hidden by the brambles, to the right of the lane, and opposite this pool all vestige of the track was lost sight of. It appeared, however, that a struggle of some nature had here taken place, and it seemed as if some large and heavy body, much larger and heavier than a man, had been drawn from the by-path to the pool. The latter was carefully dragged twice, but nothing was found; and the party were upon the point of going away, in despair of coming to any result, when Providence suggested to Mr Goodfellow the expediency of draining the water off altogether. This project was received with cheers, and many high compliments to 'Old Charley' upon his sagacity and consideration. As many of the burghers had brought spades with them, supposing that they might possibly be called upon to disinter a corpse, the drain was easily and speedily effected; and no sooner was the bottom visible, than right in the middle of the mud that remained was discovered a black silk velvet waistcoat, which nearly everyone present immediately recognised as the property of Mr Pennifeather. This waistcoat was much torn and stained with blood, and there were several persons among the party who had a distinct remembrance of its having been worn by its owner on the very morning of Mr Shuttleworthy's departure for the city; while there were others, again, ready to testify upon oath, if required, that Mr P did *not* wear the garment in question at any period during the *remainder* of that memorable day; nor could any one be found to say that he had seen it upon Mr P's person at any period at all subsequent to Mr Shuttleworthy's disappearance.

Matters now wore a very serious aspect for Mr Pennifeather, and it was observed, as an indubitable confirmation of the suspicions which were excited against him, that he grew exceedingly pale, and when asked what he

---

peculiar: distinctive
vestige: trace
Providence: Divine Guidance
expediency: advisability
sagacity and consideration: wisdom and
    thoughtfulness
disinter: dig up
subsequent to: after
indubitable confirmation: clear proof
excited: aroused

COMMENTARY
After a week, Charley's search-party finds a clue – a blood-stained silk waistcoat at the bottom of a pool. Charley is much praised for his perseverance. The waistcoat belongs to Mr Pennifeather.

had to say for himself, was utterly incapable of saying a word. Hereupon, the
few friends his riotous mode of living had left him deserted him at once to a
man, and were even more clamorous than his ancient and avowed enemies for
his instantaneous arrest. But, on the other hand, the magnanimity of Mr
Goodfellow shone forth with only the more brilliant lustre through contrast.
He made a warm and intensely eloquent defence of Mr Pennifeather, in which
he alluded more than once to his own sincere forgiveness of that wild young
gentleman – 'the heir of the worthy Mr Shuttleworthy,' – for the insult which
he (the young gentleman) had, no doubt in the heat of passion, thought
proper to put upon him (Mr Goodfellow). 'He forgave him for it,' he said,
'from the very bottom of his heart; and for himself (Mr Goodfellow), so far
from pushing the suspicious circumstances to extremity, which, he was sorry to
say, really *had* arisen against Mr Pennifeather, he (Mr Goodfellow) would make
every exertion in his power, would employ all the little eloquence in his
possession to – to – to – soften down, as much as he could conscientiously do
so, the worst features of this really exceedingly perplexing piece of business.'

Mr Goodfellow went on for some half hour longer in this strain, very much
to the credit both of his head and of his heart; but your warm-hearted people
are seldom apposite in their observations – they run into all sorts of blunders,
contre-temps and *mal apropos-isms*, in the hotheadedness of their zeal to serve a
friend – thus, often with the kindest intentions in the world, doing infinitely
more to prejudice his cause than to advance it.

So, in the present instance, it turned out with all the eloquence of 'Old
Charley'; for, although he laboured earnestly on behalf of the suspected, yet it
so happened, somehow or other, that every syllable he uttered of which the
direct but unwitting tendency was not to exalt the speaker in the good
opinion of his audience, had the effect of deepening the suspicion already
attached to the individual whose cause he pled, and of arousing against him
the fury of the mob.

One of the most unaccountable errors committed by the orator was his
allusion to the suspected as 'the heir of the worthy old gentlemen

COMMENTARY
The evidence points to Pennifeather having murdered his uncle. However, Charley
says he will do everything he can to clear the young man's name.

riotous mode of living: immoral lifestyle
clamorous: loudly in favour of
magnanimity: good-heartedness
alluded: referred
passion: anger, strong feeling
conscientiously: in good faith
strain: vein, manner
apposite in: able to live up to

contre-temps and mal apropos-isms: verbal
   errors which prevent them from
   saying what they mean
zeal: enthusiasm
earnestly: strongly
unwitting: unintentional
exalt: raise the status of
orator: speaker (i.e. Charley)

Mr Shuttleworthy.' The people had never really thought of this before. They had only remembered certain threats of disinheritance uttered a year or two previously by the uncle (who had no living relative except the nephew), and they had, therefore, always looked upon this disinheritance as a matter that was settled – so single-minded a race of beings were the Rattleburghers; but the remark of 'Old Charley' brought them at once to a consideration of this point, and thus gave them to see the possibility of the threats having been nothing *more* than a threat. And straightway, hereupon, arose the natural question of *cui bono?* – a question that tended even more than the waistcoat to fasten the terrible crime upon the young man. And here, lest I be misunderstood, permit me to digress for one moment merely to observe that the exceedingly brief and simple Latin phrase which I have employed, is invariably mistranslated and misconceived. '*Cui bono?*' in all the crack novels and elsewhere – in those of Mrs Gore, for example, (the author of 'Cecil'), a lady who quotes all tongues from the Chaldaean to Chickasaw, and is helped to her learning, 'as needed', upon a systematic plan, by Mr Beckford, – in *all* the crack novels, I say, from those of Bulwer and Dickens to those of Turnapenny and Ainsworth, the two little Latin words *cui bono* are rendered 'to what purpose?' or, (as if *quo bono*) 'to what good?' Their true meaning, nevertheless, is 'for whose advantage'. *Cui*, to whom: *bono*, is it for a benefit? It is a purely legal phrase, and applicable precisely in cases such as we have now under consideration, where the probability of the doer of a deed hinges upon the probability of the benefit accruing to this individual or to that from the deed's accomplishment. Now, in the present instance, the question of *cui bono?* very pointedly implicated Mr Pennifeather. His uncle had threatened him, after making a will in his favour, with disinheritance. But the threat had not been actually kept; the original will, it appeared, had not been altered. *Had* it been altered, the only supposable motive for murder on the part of the suspected would have been the ordinary one of revenge; and even this would have been counteracted by the hope of reinstation into the good graces of the uncle. But the will being unaltered, while the threat to alter remained suspended over the nephew's

---

disinheritance: being removed from
    Mr Shuttleworthy's will
cui bono?: to whose benefit?
misconceived: misunderstood
crack: top-notch, best-selling
accruing: being of advantage
pointedly implicated Mr Pennifeather:
    strongly indicated Pennifeather's guilt
counteracted by the hope of reinstation:
    balanced out by the hope of being
    taken back

COMMENTARY
Charley's speech has the opposite effect to the one he seems to want. When he mentions that Pennifeather, as Mr Shuttleworthy's only relative, will inherit all that his uncle has, the townspeople sense a motive for murder.

head, there appears at once the very strongest possibile inducement for the atrocity; and so concluded, very sagaciously, the worthy citizens of the borough of Rattle.

Mr Pennifeather was, accordingly, arrested upon the spot, and the crowd, after some further search, proceeded homeward, having him in custody. On the route, however, another circumstance occurred tending to confirm the suspicion entertained. Mr Goodfellow, whose zeal led him to be always a little in advance of the party, was seen suddenly to run forward a few paces, stoop and then apparently to pick up some small object from the grass. Having quickly examined it, he was observed, too, to make a sort of half attempt at concealing it in his coat pocket; but this action was noticed, as I say, and consequently prevented, when the object picked up was found to be a Spanish knife which a dozen persons at once recognised as belonging to Mr Pennifeather. Moreover, his initials were engraved upon the handle. The blade of this knife was open and bloody.

No doubt now remained of the guilt of the nephew, and immediately upon reaching Rattleborough he was taken before a magistrate for examination.

PAUSE FOR PLAYBACK:
Now look at the playback questions on page 82 before going on with your reading.

COMMENTARY
On the way home, Charley finds more evidence of Pennifeather's guilt – his bloodstained pocket knife lying in the grass. Back in Rattleborough, Pennifeather is brought before a magistrate.

inducement for the atrocity: motive for murder
entertained: generally held

Look out for…
- **the result of Pennifeather's trial.**
- **the letter that Charley receives, and what it leads to.**
- **the remarkable climax to Charley's supper party.**

Here matters again took a most unfavourable turn. The prisoner, being questioned as to his whereabouts on the morning of Mr Shuttleworthy's disappearance, had absolutely the audacity to acknowledge that on that very morning he had been out with his rifle deer-stalking, in the immediate neighbourhood of the pool where the bloodstained waistcoat had been discovered through the sagacity of Mr Goodfellow.

This latter now came forward, and, with tears in his eyes, asked permission to be examined. He said that a stern sense of the duty he owed his Maker, not less than his fellow-men, would permit him no longer to remain silent. Hitherto, the sincerest affection for the young man (notwithstanding the latter's ill treatment of himself, Mr Goodfellow) had induced him to make every hypothesis which imagination could suggest, by way of endeavouring to account for what appeared suspicious in the circumstances that told so seriously against Mr Pennifeather; but these circumstances were now altogether *too* convincing – *too* damning; he would hesitate no longer – he would tell all he knew, although his heart (Mr Goodfellow's) should absolutely burst asunder in the effort. He then went on to state that, on the afternoon of the day previous to Mr Shuttleworthy's departure for the city, that worthy old gentleman had mentioned to his nephew, in *his* hearing (Mr Goodfellow's), that his object of going to town on the morrow was to make a deposit of an unusually large sum of money in the 'Farmers and Mechanics' Bank', and that, then and there, the said Mr Shuttleworthy had distinctly avowed to the said nephew his irrevocable determination of rescinding the will originally made,

audacity: bare-faced cheek
be examined: i.e. be called as a witness
Hitherto: Up to now
hypothesis: theory
burst asunder: break in two
irrevocable: unchangeable
rescinding: cancelling

COMMENTARY
The magistrate's hearing begins badly for Pennifeather. On the morning of his uncle's disappearance, he was out shooting near the pool where his waistcoat was found. Charley's testimony shows that he had yet another motive for murder.

and of cutting him off without a shilling. He (the witness) now solemnly called upon the accused to state whether what he (the witness) had just stated was or was not the truth in every substantial particular. Much to the astonishment of every one present, Mr Pennifeather frankly admitted that *it was*.

The magistrate now considered it his duty to send a couple of constables to search the chamber of the accused in the house of his uncle. From this search they almost immediately returned with the well-known steel-bound, russet leather pocket-book which the old gentleman had been in the habit of carrying for years. Its valuable contents, however, had been abstracted, and the magistrate in vain endeavoured to extort from the prisoner the use which had been made of them, or the place of their concealment. Indeed, he obstinately denied all knowledge of the matter. The constables, also, discovered, between the bed and sacking of the unhappy man, a shirt and neck-handkerchief both marked with the initials of his name, and both hideously besmeared with the blood of the victim.

At this juncture, it was announced that the horse of the murdered man has just expired in the stable from the effects of the wound he had received, and it was proposed by Mr Goodfellow that a *post-mortem* examination of the beast should be immediately made, with the view, if possible, of discovering the ball. This was accordingly done; and, as if to demonstrate beyond a question the guilt of the accused, Mr Goodfellow, after considerable searching in the cavity of the chest, was enabled to detect and to pull forth a bullet of very extraordinary size, which, upon trial, was found to be exactly adapted to the bore of Mr Pennifeather's rifle, while it was far too large for that of any other person in the borough or its vicinity. To render the matter even surer yet, however, this bullet was discovered to have a flaw or seam at right angles to the usual suture; and upon examination, this seam corresponded precisely with an accidental ridge or elevation in a pair of moulds acknowledged by the accused himself to be his own property. Upon the finding of this bullet, the examining magistrate refused to listen to any further testimony, and immediately committed the prisoner to trial –

COMMENTARY
Evidence against Pennifeather continues to mount. Mr Shuttleworthy's empty wallet is found in Pennifeather's room. Mr Shuttleworthy's horse dies, and a post-mortem is carried out on it to find the bullet which killed it.

substantial particular: important detail
russet: reddish-brown
abstracted: removed
expired: died
ball: bullet
suture: join

declining resolutely to take any bail in the case, although against this severity Mr Goodfellow very warmly remonstrated, and offered to become surety in whatever amount might be required. This generosity on the part of 'Old Charley' was only in accordance with the whole tenor of his amiable and chivalrous conduct during the entire period of his sojourn in the borough of Rattle. In the present instance, the worthy man was so entirely carried away by the excessive warmth of his sympathy, that he seemed to have quite forgotten, when he offered to go bail for his young friend, that he himself (Mr Goodfellow) did not possess a single dollar's worth of property upon the face of the earth.

The result of the committal may be readily foreseen. Mr Pennifeather, amid the loud execrations of all Rattleborough, was brought to trial at the next criminal sessions, when the chain of circumstantial evidence (strengthened as it was by some additional damning facts, which Mr Goodfellow's sensitive conscientiousness forbade him to withhold from the court) was considered so unbroken and so thoroughly conclusive, that the jury, without leaving their seats, returned an immediate verdict of '*Guilty of murder in the first degree.*' Soon afterward the unhappy wretch received sentence of death, and was remanded to the county jail to await the inexorable vengeance of the law.

In the meantime, the noble behaviour of 'Old Charley Goodfellow' had doubly endeared him to the honest citizens of the borough. He became ten times a greater favourite than ever; and, as a natural result of the hospitality with which he was treated, he relaxed, as it were, perforce, the extremely parsimonious habits which his poverty had hitherto impelled him to observe, and very frequently had little *réunions* at his own house, when wit and jollity reigned supreme – dampened a little, *of course*, by the occasional remembrance of the untoward and melancholy fate which impended over the nephew of the late lamented bosom friend of the generous host.

One fine day, this magnanimous old gentleman was agreeably surprised at the receipt of the following letter:–

declining resolutely: refusing sternly
severity: harsh decision
remonstrated: protested
become surety: put up the bail money
tenor: tone, nature
amiable and chivalrous conduct: kind and
    public-spirited behaviour
sojourn: stay
execrations: curses
inexorable: relentless
parsimonious: thrifty
untoward: untimely
magnanimous: kind-hearted

COMMENTARY
Pennifeather is put on trial, found guilty and sentenced to death. The people of Rattleborough hail Charley as a champion of justice – almost single-handed, he has uncovered the nephew's treacherous murder plot.

'Charles Goodfellow, Esquire –

'Dear Sir – In conformity with an order transmitted to our firm about two months since, by our esteemed correspondent, Mr Barnabas Shuttleworthy, we have the honour of forwarding this morning, to your address, a double box of Château Margaux of the antelope brand, violet seal. Box numbered and marked as per margin.

'We remain, sir,
'Your most ob'nt ser'ts
'HOGGS, FROGS, BOGS & CO.

'City of ——, June 21, 18—.

P.S. – The box will reach you, by wagon, on the day after your receipt of this letter. Our respects to Mr Shuttleworthy.
H. F. B. & Co'

Charles Goodfellow Esq., Rattleborough.
From H. F. B. & Co.
Chat. Mar. A – No. 1 – 6 doz. bottles ($\frac{1}{2}$ Gross)

The fact is, that Mr Goodfellow had, since the death of Mr Shuttleworthy, given over all expectation of ever receiving the promised Château Margaux; and he, therefore, looked upon it *now* as a sort of especial dispensation of Providence in his behalf. He was highly delighted, of course, and in the exuberance of his joy invited a large party of friends to a *petit souper* on the morrow, for the purpose of broaching the good old Mr Shuttleworthy's present. Not that he *said* anything about 'the good old Mr Shuttleworthy' when he issued the invitations. The fact is, he thought much and concluded to say nothing at all. He did *not* mention to any one – if I remember aright – that he had received a *present* of Château Margaux. He merely asked his friends to come and help him drink some of a remarkably fine quality and rich flavour that he had ordered up from the city a couple of months ago, and of which he

COMMENTARY
Charley receives a letter from a wine-merchant. He has quite forgotten that Mr Shuttleworthy promised him, as a present, a double box of his favourite wine. Six dozen bottles will be delivered the following day.

dispensation: gift, reward
petit souper: supper party
broaching: opening

would be in the receipt upon the morrow. I have often puzzled myself to imagine *why* it was that 'Old Charley' came to the conclusion to say nothing about having received the wine from his old friend, but I could never precisely understand his reason for the silence, although he had *some* excellent and very magnanimous reason, no doubt.

The morrow at length arrived, and with it a very large and highly respectable company at Mr Goodfellow's house. Indeed, half the borough was there, – I myself among the number, – but, much to the vexation of the host, the Château Margaux did not arrive until a late hour, and when the sumptuous supper supplied by 'Old Charley' had been done very ample justice by the guests. It came at length, however, – a monstrously big box of it there was, too, – and as the whole party were in excessively good humour, it was decided, *nem. con.*, that it should be lifted upon the table and its contents disembowelled forthwith.

No sooner said than done. I lent a helping hand; and, in a trice, we had the box upon the table, in the midst of all the bottles and glasses, not a few of which were demolished in the scuffle. 'Old Charley', who was pretty much intoxicated, and excessively red in the face, now took a seat, with an air of mock dignity, at the head of the board, and thumped furiously upon it with a decanter, calling upon the company to keep order 'during the ceremony of disinterring the treasure.'

After some vociferation, quiet was at length restored, and, as very often happens in similar cases, a profound and remarkable silence ensued. Being then requested to force open the lid, I complied, of course, 'with an infinite deal of pleasure.' I inserted a chisel, and giving it a few slight taps with a hammer, the top of the box flew suddenly off, and, at the same instant, there sprang up into a sitting position, directly facing the host, the bruised, bloody, and nearly putrid corpse of the murdered Mr Shuttleworthy himself. It gazed for a few moments, fixedly and sorrowfully, with its decaying and lack-lustre eyes full into the countenance of Mr Goodfellow; uttered slowly, but clearly and impressively the words – 'Thou art the man!' and then, falling over the

nem. con.: unanimously
board: table
vociferation: excited chatter
ensued: followed
complied: agreed
putrid: rotten, decomposed
lack-lustre: dull, lifeless
countenance: face

COMMENTARY
To help him celebrate, Charley invites a great many friends and neighbours to supper. They enjoy a splendid meal, during which the box of wine arrives. Everyone agrees to open it there and then. From the box rises the corpse of Mr Shuttleworthy. In front of the guests, it accuses Charley of his murder.

side of the chest as if thoroughly satisfied, stretched out its limbs quiveringly upon the table.

The scene that ensued is altogether beyond description. The rush for the doors and windows was terrific, and many of the most robust men in the room fainted outright through sheer horror. But after the first, wild, shrieking burst of affright, all eyes were directed to Mr Goodfellow. If I live a thousand years, I can never forget the more than mortal agony which was depicted in that ghastly face of his, so lately rubicund with triumph and wine. For several minutes he sat rigidly as a statue of marble; his eyes seeming, in the intense vacancy of their gaze, to be turned inward and absorbed in the contemplation of his own miserable, murderous soul. At length their expression appeared to flash suddenly out into the external world, when, with a quick leap, he sprang from his chair, and falling heavily with his head and shoulders upon the table, and in contact with the corpse, poured out rapidly and vehemently a detailed confession of the hideous crime for which Mr Pennifeather was then imprisoned and doomed to die.

What he recounted was in substance this –

He followed his victim to the vicinity of the pool; there shot his horse with a pistol; despatched its rider with the butt end; possessed himself of the pocket-book; and, supposing the horse dead, dragged it with great labour to the brambles by the pond. Upon his own beast he slung the corpse of Mr Shuttleworthy, and thus bore it to a secure place of concealment a long distance off through the woods.

The waistcoat, the knife, the pocket-book, and bullet, had been placed by himself where found, with the view to avenging himself upon Mr Pennifeather. He has also contrived the discovery of the stained handkerchief and shirt.

Toward the end of the blood-chilling recital, the words of the guilty wretch faltered and grew hollow. When the record was finally exhausted, he arose, staggered backward from the table, and fell – *dead*.

The means by which this happily-timed confession was extorted, although

COMMENTARY

Corpses don't lie: everyone is aghast. As if caught in a nightmare, Charley begins to confess how he did it. After ending his confession, he collapses and dies.

robust: strong-hearted
rubicund: flushed
vacancy: emptiness
vehemently: passionately
in substance: briefly
despatched: put to death
contrived: arranged
extorted: brought to light

efficient, were simple indeed. Mr Goodfellow's excess of frankness had disgusted me, and excited my suspicions from the first. I was present when Mr Pennifeather had struck him, and the fiendish expression which then arose upon his countenance, although momentary, assured me that his threat of vengeance would, if possible, be rigidly fulfilled. I was thus prepared to view the *manoeuvring* of 'Old Charley' in a very different light from that in which it was regarded by the good citizens of Rattleborough. I saw at once that all the criminating discoveries arose, either directly or indirectly, from himself. But the fact which clearly opened my eyes to the true state of the case, was the affair of the bullet, *found* by Mr G. in the carcass of the horse. *I* had not forgotten, although the Rattleburghers *had*, that there was a hole where the ball had entered the horse, and another where it *went out*. If it were found in the animal then, after having made its exit, I saw clearly that it must have been deposited by the person who found it. The bloody shirt and handkerchief confirmed the idea suggested by the bullet; for the blood on examination proved to be capital claret, and no more. When I came to think of these things, and also of the late increase of liberality and expenditure on the part of Mr Goodfellow, I entertained a suspicion which was none the less strong because I kept it altogether to myself.

In the meantime, I instituted a rigorous private search for the corpse of Mr Shuttleworthy, and, for good reasons, searched in quarters as divergent as possible from those to which Mr Goodfellow conducted his party. The result was that, after some days, I came across an old dry well, the mouth of which was nearly hidden by brambles; and here, at the bottom, I discovered what I sought.

Now it so happened that I had overheard the colloquy between the two cronies, when Mr Goodfellow had contrived to cajole his host into the promise of a box of Château Margaux. Upon this hint I acted. I procured a stiff piece of whalebone, thrust it down the throat of the corpse, and deposited the latter in an old wine box – taking care so to double the body up as to double the whalebone with it. In this manner I had to press forcibly upon the lid to keep

---

frankness: honesty and 'goodness'
fiendish: wicked, dangerous
criminating discoveries: clues pointing to
   Pennifeather's guilt
capital claret: fine red wine
rigorous: thorough
divergent: different
colloquy: conversation
cajole: persuade by flattery
procured: obtained

COMMENTARY

The narrator concludes the story by looking back at the mistakes Charley made while trying to 'frame' Pennifeather. He explains how, by himself, he found Mr Shuttleworthy's corpse – and how he arranged for it to sit up and 'speak' at Charley's supper party.

it down while I secured it with nails; and I anticipated, of course, that as soon as these latter were removed, the top would fly *off* and the body *up*.

Having thus arranged the box, I marked, numbered, and addressed it as already told; and then writing a letter in the name of the wine-merchants with whom Mr Shuttleworthy dealt, I gave instructions to my servant to wheel the box to Mr Goodfellow's door, in a barrow, at a given signal from myself. For the words which I intended the corpse to speak, I confidently depended on my ventriloquial abilities; for their effect, I counted upon the conscience of the murderous wretch.

I believe there is nothing more to be explained. Mr Pennifeather was released upon the spot, inherited the fortune of his uncle, profited by the lessons of experience, turned over a new leaf, and led happily ever afterward a new life.

PAUSE FOR PLAYBACK:
Now look at the playback questions on page 82.

COMMENTARY
Pennifeather is released and, with the help of his uncle's inheritance, goes on to live a blameless life.

ventriloquial abilities: skill at 'throwing' my voice

Study guide

PAGES 65 TO 73:

- ➤ How long, exactly, has Charley Goodfellow been living in Rattleborough? What are we told about his former life?
- ➤ In the search for Mr Shuttleworthy's body, two pieces of evidence are found to link Pennifeather with his murder. What are they? Who finds them?
- ➤ What fate do you think awaits Pennifeather in the rest of the story?
- ➤ Mr Shuttleworthy's body has not yet been found. What do *you* think has happened to it?

Now return to reading the story on page 74

PAGES 74 TO 81:

- ➤ When Pennifeather is 'brought to trial', how do the townspeople react? Is this typical of them?
- ➤ The jury find Pennifeather '*Guilty of murder in the first degree*' 'without leaving their seats' – that is, without discussing the evidence. Why do you think they are so sure of their verdict?
- ➤ Near the end, the narrator becomes a character in the story he is telling. Whereabouts, exactly? Why do you think Poe needs to do this?
- ➤ In reading through the story, did *you* reach the same conclusion as the narrator did? If so, at what point?

REVIEWING THE WHOLE STORY: SUGGESTED ACTIVITIES

1 Host Dies After Corpse Joins In Supper Party! A front-page story

The editor of *The Rattleborough Record* is one of the guests at Charley's supper party. Next day, the front page carries a 'sensational story' about what happened there. In this activity, you are the editor responsible for writing the front page.

a **By yourself**, check your facts by re-reading the account of the supper party. Bear in mind you do not know that the narrator 'arranged' a little surprise for Charley: you are reporting what you saw with your own eyes.

Make notes about what to include in your report – and how you intend to present it.

b *The Rattleborough Record* is a tabloid newspaper. The story you have to tell, therefore, is the answer to an editor's prayer. Make the most of it; not much happens in Rattleborough normally. Before drafting your story, look at some recent front pages from tabloid newspapers of the present day. Imagine how *they* would report this story. Consider in particular:

- headlines and sub-headlines, and how they make their impact.

- the use of illustrations and accompanying captions.

- the way in which different type-faces are used.

- how interviews and 'quotes' feature prominently.

- how the whole page is set out.

- above all, the vocabulary and style used by a tabloid reporter.

c Now draft your story. When you have finished, **join up with a partner**. Take it in turns to read your draft versions to each other *aloud*, using a suitable tone of voice. Then read your partner's draft to yourself.

Comment on (i) how true to the facts the story is and (ii) how successfully it imitates the style and lay-out of a typical tabloid.

d **By yourself**, write your front page in 'best' form. Try to make it look as much like the real thing as possible. If you wish, use a computer.

2 | Snake in the grass

It is Charley, not Pennifeather, who turns out to have been playing a treacherous 'double game'. This activity asks you to uncover Charley's plot to pin the blame on, or 'frame', Pennifeather – and to explain it in a full, clearly detailed way.

a   **In a group**, look back over the whole story. Talk about (i) why Charley murders Mr Shuttleworthy and (ii) all the ways in which he tries to frame Pennifeather. To help you, each make a 'framing chart', like this:

Charley's action	Intended effect	How he managed it
1. Suggests draining the pool	To find P's waistcoat there	Planted the waistcoat earlier
2 Finds P's pocket-knife in the grass	?	?

You should be able to make *ten* or more entries on your chart.

b   **Join up with another group**. Compare your findings. In particular, talk about 'how he managed it'. In some cases, you will have to read between the lines and work from clues dropped in the story, since the narrator does not explain *everything* that Charley did.

If members of the other group have found points that you haven't, add them to your chart.

c   **By yourself**, imagine you are the narrator at the end of the story. You will be called to give evidence at the post mortem into Charley's death. There you decide to reveal all you know about Charley's 'double game' with Pennifeather. Use your framing chart to help you plan out what you are going to say and the order in which you are going to say it.

Now make a choice. You can either write a statement to be read out at the post mortem on your behalf – or you can use your notes to act out what you say in person. If you choose the latter, **join up with a partner** who has decided to do the same. Take it in turns to play the roles of the narrator and the coroner at the post mortem. The coroner will question you in the course of your evidence.

If you opt for the role-play, your teacher may wish to use this activity to assess your Speaking and Listening skills.

3 Making the difference

'Thou Art the Man' has been included in this volume partly because it differs, in several respects, from the stories that come before it. In this activity, you are asked to examine what these differences are – and to reach your own judgement about whether the story is an effective one.

a **As a class**, remind yourselves of any other Poe story you have read in this volume. Briefly discuss:

- what kind of *plot* (or story-line) does it have – and what gives rise to the events in it?

- what is its main *theme*: that is, what ideas is Poe most interested in?

- what is its *setting*: that is, where does the action take place?

- what sort of *atmosphere* does it have?

- is it, in your opinion, a good story – and, if so, why?

b **In a group**, compare 'Thou Art the Man' with the story you have discussed as a class.

First, note down any *similarities* you find. For instance, would it be true to say that what happens at the supper party is 'typical Poe'?

Next, note down the main *differences* you can see, using the following headings in relation to 'Thou Art the Man':

> 1 **What does the plot depend on?**
> 2 **Where is the story set?**
> 3 **How would you describe the general tone of the story?**
> 4 **Who tells the story, and in what sort of style?**
> 5 **How does Poe try to keep us entertained?**

c **As a class**, share your ideas about the differences you have discussed. Quote from both stories to back up the points you make.

Finally, consider how effective and entertaining one story is compared with the other. If necessary, your teacher will help you decide how to come to your own conclusions.

d **By yourself**, use all the work you have done during this activity to write a comparison between 'Thou Art the Man' and any other of Poe's stories. Use quotations wherever you feel they help you to make your ideas clear.

Overview

The activities in this section ask you to do two things:

1   Talk and/or write about the stories in order to understand more about the way they are told.

You will be looking at:

- **Narrative**   The way a story is built up and organised.

- **Characterisation**   The way the characters are presented to us.

- **Themes**   The main ideas and issues the author writes about.

- **Setting and atmosphere**   The importance of particular places and how they are described in a story.

2   Make comparisons between some of the stories.

1 Vengeance is mine!

In all five stories in this volume, the theme of revenge is prominent. **As a class**, or **in groups**, compare the use Poe makes of a 'revenge plot' in any two stories.

Points to consider

- In *Hop-Frog*, why do the dwarfs want revenge on the king? Do you think they are justified in going to the lengths they do to achieve it?

- In *The Tell-Tale Heart*, how does the murderer's revenge on the old man with the 'Evil Eye' backfire against him? In your opinion, does he deserve what he gets?

- In *The Masque of the Red Death*, how could the 'Red Death' figure be seen to be taking revenge on Prince Prospero and his guests? What is your idea of the moral (or message) of this story?

- In *The Cask of Amontillado*, the narrator's 'revenge' against Fortunato seems to be without motive. Do you think this adds to, or takes away from, the effectiveness of the story?

- In *'Thou Art the Man'*, how cleverly does the narrator take revenge against Charley Goodfellow? Is he acting mainly for himself, or for others?

- How far do you agree that a story based on revenge – as opposed to, say, romance, mystery, science fiction, crime detection, etc. – is more likely to contain the following elements:

    • hatred   • cruelty   • violence   • madness   • death?

    To what extent do the stories you are discussing depend upon some or all of these?

Suggestions for writing

a   Compare any two characters from different stories in their roles as revengers. With which of them do you feel more sympathy, and why?

b   'Poe wrote so often about revenge because it gave him an opportunity to include more horror in his stories'. How far do you agree? Refer to at least two stories in support of your view.

2 | What kind of characters?

It has been said that the characters in Poe's stories are not recognisable people but 'studies of extreme and disturbed states of minds'.

As a class, or **in groups**, consider the truth of this statement by applying it to two or three characters from different stories.

Points to consider

- In most stories, we find out about a character's background and how s/he fits into the society to which s/he belongs. How true is this of Poe's characters?

- In stories like *The Tell-Tale Heart* and *The Cask of Amontillado*, the main characters speak in their own voices. How much do they tell us about *themselves*? By the end of the story, how well do we understand the kind of people they are?

- In most stories, we learn about a character partly (or largely) through his/her *relationships* with others. Is this true of the characters in Poe's stories?

- In any or all of these stories, which do you think is more important: what the characters are really like – or the atmosphere of mystery, horror and the grotesque which Poe creates through them?

- Take the particular characters you are considering in turn. Imagine that you had to compose an obituary for each of them. What would you be able to say? Try writing the first paragraph.

Suggestions for writing

a   Compare *two* characters from different stories. To what extent, and in what ways, would you say they exhibit a 'disturbed' state of mind?

b   'Poe is not interested in the relationships between people. What concerns him is their personal psychology and their "inner lives".' Using *two* or *three* characters as examples, consider the truth of this statement.

3 Comparing styles

Below are two extracts from Poe stories not printed in this volume. **As a class**, or **in groups**, read the extracts closely. Then compare the style in which they are written with any of the stories you have read.

Extract 1

During the whole of a dull, dark and soundless day in the autumn of the year, when the clouds hung oppressively low in the heavens, I had been passing alone, on horseback, through a singularly dreary tract of country, and at length found myself, as the shades of the evening drew on, within view of the melancholy House of Usher. I know now how it was – but, with the first glimpse of the building, a sense of insufferable gloom pervaded my spirit. I say insufferable; for the feeling was unrelieved by any of that half-pleasurable, because poetic, sentiment with which the mind usually receives even the sternest natural images of the desolate or the terrible. I looked upon the scene before me – upon the mere house, and the simple landscape features of the domain – upon the bleak walls – upon the vacant eye-like windows – upon a few rank sedges – and upon a few white trunks of decayed trees – with an utter depression of soul which I can compare to no earthly sensation more properly than to the after-dream of the reveller upon opium – the bitter lapse into every-day life – the hideous dropping off of the veil. There was an iciness, a sinking, a sickening of the heart – an unredeemed dreariness of thought which no goading of the imagination could torture into aught of the sublime. What was it – I paused to think – what was it that so unnerved me in the contemplation of the House of Usher?

(from *The Fall of the House of Usher*)

Extract 2

The heat rapidly increased, and once again I looked up, shuddering as with a fit of ague. There had been a second change in the cell – and now the change was obviously in the *form*. As before, it was in vain that I at first endeavoured to appreciate or understand what was taking place. But not long was I left in doubt. The Inquisitorial vengeance had been hurried by my two-fold escape, and there was to be no more dallying with the King of Terrors. The room had been square. I saw that two of its iron angles were now acute – two, consequently, obtuse. The fearful difference quickly increased with a low rumbling or moaning sound. In an instant the apartment had shifted its form into that of a lozenge. But the alteration stopped not here – I neither hoped nor desired it to stop. I could have clasped the red walls to my bosom as a garment of eternal peace. 'Death,' I said, 'any death but that of the pit!' Fool! might I not have known that *into the pit* it was the object of the burning iron to urge me? Could I resist its glow? or if even that, could I withstand its pressure? And now, flatter and flatter grew the lozenge, with a rapidity that left me no time for contemplation. Its centre, and of course its greatest width, came just over the yawning gulf. I shrank back – but the closing walls pressed me resistlessly onward. At length for my seared and writhing body there was no longer an inch of foothold on the firm floor of the prison. I struggled no more, but the agony of my soul found vent in one loud, long, and final scream

of despair. I felt that I tottered upon the brink – I averted my eyes – .
There was a discordant hum of human voices! There was a loud blast as of many
trumpets! There was a harsh grating as of a thousand thunders! The fiery walls
rushed back! An outstretched arm caught my own as I fell, fainting, into the
abyss. It was that of General Lasalle. The French army had entered Toledo. The
Inquisition was in the hands of its enemies.

(from *The Pit and the Pendulum*)

Points to consider

- Think of other stories by Poe you have read in this volume. **As a class**,
  make a list of all the elements in these two extracts which suggest that
  their author is, unmistakably, Edgar Allan Poe.

- Look closely at Extract 1. How would you describe its atmosphere or
  'mood'? Pick out the single words and phrases which help create this
  atmosphere most strongly.

- Do the same with Extract 2.

- Select *two* complete sentences from each extract. Talk about how Poe
  constructs them in such a way as to hold your interest in what he is
  describing.

Suggestions for writing

a   Write a commentary on one or both of the extracts above, showing how
    Poe's choice of language creates a powerful atmosphere.

b   Referring to the extracts above and to any of the stories in this volume,
    give your views on what is most distinctive about the style in which Poe
    writes.

4 | Horror struck again

Whether or not you have worked on *Hop-Frog*, turn back to Activity 5 on
page 24.

As a class, or **in groups**, use the diagram and the 'score card' to discuss (i)
the common elements in at least *two* horror stories in this volume, and (ii) how
successful you judge them to be.

By yourself, write a comparison between *one* of Poe's horror stories and *one*
by another author. Modern writers such as Stephen King, Angela Carter or
Dennis Wheatley would be suitable choices. If you wish, however, compare
Poe with an author from earlier times – for example, Bram Stoker, Mary
Shelley, H. P. Lovecraft.

If you choose a modern author, try to say how much you feel s/he has been influenced by Poe – and how successful a 'horror' writer s/he is in comparison with him.

5 | The story of a life

It is often said that Poe's most remarkable story was his own life. Read, or re-read, the brief biography of him on pages 2 to 3 of this volume.

By yourself, use this as a starting-point for your own further research. Your teacher will offer suggestions about sources of information. Perhaps the fullest and most reliable account of Poe's life is *The Tell-Tale Heart* by Julian Symons.

Choose one part of Poe's life you find particularly interesting. Write about it as if it were one of his own stories. Use a style which resembles that of any of the stories in this volume, or of any listed in the Introduction on page 3.